CW00410577

SAVING THE WRETCHED SLUM GIRL

ELLA CORNISH

This is a work of fiction. Any names or characters, businesses or places, events or incidents, are fictitious. Any resemblance to actual persons, living or dead, or actual events is purely coincidental.

Copyright © 2022 by Ella Cornish

All rights reserved.

No part of this book may be reproduced in any form or by any electronic or mechanical means, including information storage and retrieval systems, without written permission from the author, except for the use of brief quotations in a book review.

Email: ellacornishauthor@gmail.com

CHAPTER 1

*S*even-year-old Alice Smythe was small for her age, which in some ways was a bonus as it allowed her to work as a scavenger mule at the Langford Cotton Mill, in the East End of London. She and her mother had worked there together for the past six months, Alice having commenced her employment at the mill the day after her seventh birthday.

They toiled from dawn till dusk often not seeing the outside light during the day at all. She listened intently to the clacking of the machinery as it moved back and forth, the spindle catching the yarn at the top and winding it up, as if it were a spinning top she had seen once at the travelling fair.

Alice needed to be careful when she scrambled underneath, she knew the work was dangerous—her mother had reminded her many times—but her family needed the money to survive. The loud deafening sound of the busy machinery no longer hurt her ears as it had in her first few months, her mother had told her to push some cotton fluff in them to dull the noise and she wore a remnant of cloth across her mouth to keep the loose threads and cotton dust from clogging up her throat and lungs.

Her mother suffered from a nasty cough, brought on by years of working in the hot, humid conditions that were needed in a cotton mill. She would hear her in the middle of the night getting up gasping for air, drinking to try and relieve the spasms, but nothing seemed to help. Her cough was getting much worse but still she needed to work else they would end up in the workhouse and that would be dishonourable beyond words. No one ever wanted to end up there, it would be a disgrace.

As quick as a mouse, she darted under the dangerous mechanical movement, keeping her head low, almost touching the filthy wooden floor as she gathered up the loose cotton balls that had fallen from the equipment. Her small nimble fingers tucked them into the pocket of the dark apron that her mother had placed around her waist just this morning. Dashing forward before the machine could complete another turn, Alice darted out on the other side—she was safe this time.

Even at the young age of seven, Alice knew that there was a heavy risk around the machines. Her mother would warn her several times a day to be careful about watching her head and keeping her wits about her at all times. While she didn't enjoy the task she had been given, Alice knew that her family badly needed the extra money now that her father wasn't able to work. It was up to Alice and her mother, Mary to find the necessary finances to support them. They were luckier than some, she was an only child, Alice couldn't imagine how hard it must be for families with several children.

Alice hurried around the machine, placing the loose cotton scraps into the storage barrel that would be taken away at the end of the day, dumping the oddments into the large vats of leftover fragments. Alice liked the way the soft cotton felt between her fingertips. Just the other day she had put some in her pocket and taken it home, keeping it under her pillow to touch in the cold dark nights. She would have been whipped by Master Turney, the foreman, if he had found out, but Alice hadn't been forced to empty her pockets that particular day, so no one knew and now she had something of her own that no one else knew about.

Not even her mother…

"Alice! Stop daydreaming. The cotton isn't going to pick itself up!"

Her mother's voice cut through her thoughts and Alice darted under the machine once more, gathering up the cotton. A few strands of fine blonde hair clung to Alice's moist neck as she quickly finished her task. Her mother made her wear a dark brown mop cap so that her hair wouldn't get trapped in the constantly moving machinery above her head, telling her daughter that she had seen it happen once, that a little girl had been scalped before they could stop the machines. All of Alice's clothes were either brown or black in colour, her mother insisted that she wear dark clothing. After all, you couldn't see the dirt if it was the same colour as the material, she would say.

"Smythe!"

Alice cringed at the sound of Master Turney's shrill voice, scurrying out of his path as he bared down on her mother. Having worked at the Langford Cotton Mill for most of her life, her mother didn't even flinch at the man's putrid breath hovering over her. "Yes, Master Turney?" she answered plainly.

He pointed at Alice, who was peeking out from behind one of the machines. "Why isn't your gel sweeping the floor like she is paid to do?" the man growled angrily.

"I will have her do it straightaway, Master Turney," her mother replied. Alice didn't waste any time finding the broom. Hurrying as far away as possible from the conversation, she set to sweeping up the dust and cotton fragments too small to be picked up. She didn't like Master Turney and very few workers at the factory did. He was a nasty vicious bully, who wouldn't think twice about using his fists to get what he wanted.

Her small body moved the broom furiously over the grimy floor, causing a small cloud of dust to rise which tickled her nose through her face covering, but she managed not to sneeze. In the near distance, she saw a familiar face, nine-year-old John Cartwright, walking through the hallway. It was unbelievable that he was back at work so soon after his terrible accident.

He was one of the piecers, a job known to be very dangerous, and John had proved the point. He had not been in work for the past few days. Alice remembered back to the day when John had been hurt, she had never seen so much blood before in her young life and, despite the fact that her mother had tried to shield her from it, Alice had still seen enough of the carnage to scare her for a lifetime.

Poor John had got his hand caught trying to repair the broken threads, he had foolishly tried to grab his cap that had been dislodged because he was growing too tall.

"What's he doin' here, he canna work like that?" the foreman shouted above the roar of the machines. "Look at that bandage, there's still blood seeping through."

"I promise ye he can still work, just as well. He's a strong lad. Put him on moving the barrels or helping with sweeping the floors. Please, I beg of ye," his mother, Myrtle pleaded. She was a thin scraggy woman and most folks in the factory knew that John and Myrtle depended on the work to support his younger siblings. His father had passed just five months ago from the same cough that Alice's poor mother was displaying.

Alice swallowed as her eyes trailed towards the bandage, gasping when she realised that it was evident that two of his fingers were not where they should be.

Shaking his head, Turney relented, sending John to the docking area where the cotton came in to be sent to the looms, yelling for the trembling woman to get back to her work too. The rest of the day passed by slowly and without incident and by the time the sun was starting to fade through the filth ingrained windows, Alice's hands were covered in fresh bulging blisters from holding the broom far too tightly.

Passing down the last aisle, she swept the dust away from the pathways between the looms. Just as she was finishing up, she heard raised voices and crept a little closer to the sound.

"I don't care what you were doing! You weren't here, Nicholas! That is all that matters. I want you here and in *my* bed at night."

"Now, you listen to me, I had business to attend to, Catherine. You couldn't possibly understand what I was doing."

Alice took a quick peek in the direction the voices were coming from, her eyes widening, when she saw the owner of the Mill, Mr Nicholas Langford, standing close by, next to his wife, Catherine Langford. Mr Langford was dressed in a fine dark charcoal grey suit, the shiny golden chain of a pocket watch swaying across the front of his rather portly stomach that was covered by colourful floral waistcoat. Catherine Langford was dressed in a gown that was perhaps the loveliest that Alice had ever seen, having a deep crimson colour with pretty cream coloured lacework at the neck and cuffs. Alice wondered if the material felt as soft and smooth as it looked.

She would never attempt to touch the fabric, however, that would never do, it would be cause for instant dismissal. She could see that Catherine Langford was annoyed as she glared angrily at her husband. Alice had seen that stance many times before. It was the same one that her mother liked to use when Alice was misbehaving. She was intrigued to know what was going on and she couldn't help but stand stock still and gawp as the couple continued to argue.

"Oh, Nicholas, I'm well aware of what you were doing," Catherine Langford said, her hands flying about wildly. "You were with that hussy again, weren't you?"

Mr Langford stepped forward, hands raised as he tried to placate his angry wife. "Come, come, you don't know what you are talking about."

Catherine Langford laughed audibly and there was a bitterness to the high-pitched sound. "Oh, Nicholas, I am not as naïve as you may think. I know you have a mistress and have done for some time." Alice gasped at the woman's strange words. She knew she shouldn't continue to listen to another's private conversation, but she simply couldn't help herself. Catherine Langford continued speaking, her voice a little lower now. "That is not why I sought you out though. Our son, Matthew, is due to return from school for the summer break. I expect he will be going back at the start of the autumn term."

"Mm-hm," Nicholas acknowledged, clearing his throat. "I'm not sure that is a good idea. I suggest he comes to work in the mill so he can come to understand some of what he is destined to inherit. It's about time he learnt the family trade. That's how I learnt the goings on of this establishment—from my father, not by spending money on an expensive education."

"I understand, but he will still be returning to school to finish his education. I insist," Mrs Langford stated plainly, pushing her index finger into the man's chest to prove her point. "He's destined for greatness. He may not have a title, but that does not matter in this time of vast economic growth."

"As you well know, my darling," the man replied, a cruel sneer spreading across his face. "This is our livelihood. It is what pays for your fancy gowns and afternoon teas with those simpering women you call your friends. Of course, he will finish the necessary education but then he is expected to learn how to run this factory. Too much of a fancy education isn't going to help without the practical experience to help him get on in life."

Catherine Langford didn't look as if she was about to back down and Alice waited to see what the man would do next. "As long as you allow him to complete his studies, I will be satisfied," she said placing her hands firmly on her hips. "But you are not to renege on your word."

"S'cuse me, Mr Langford. We need to talk about them workers and which ones ain't pulling their weight and what we need to do about 'em?"

The couple turned as Master Turney approached them, causing Alice to shrink back into the shadows, her young mind attempting to sort out the conversation she had just overheard. So, the owner had a son, one that she was not aware of. What good fortune he had, never needing to work in this grimy, dirt-laden mill but going to school to learn to read and write, something she had always dreamt of doing.

Sighing with frustration, she quickly finished her work before making her way back to her mother. "Ready, my darling gel?" her mother asked trying to smother a cough, tightening the scarf around her head and handing Alice her coat. "There is a cold wind out there. We wouldn't want to catch our deaths, so button up and come along with me," she continued holding out her hand for Alice to take.

Alice donned her coat and thin woollen scarf before making their way down the stone steps with the other workers, their workday finally at an end. Alice stayed close to her mother as they exited the mill, grasping her hand lightly. The lamp lighters were already out, lighting the smoggy streets, allowing them a dull glow with which to find their way home. By the time they got back, Alice's nose was red and streaming from the cold.

Her father eagerly awaited them inside, leaning heavily on his crutch as they entered in a flurry. "There you are," he cried as Alice shrugged out of her coat. "I have made us some dinner."

Her mother gave him a grateful smile, knowing that there was little food to be had and it would have been difficult to cook something nourishing for them all. "That was kind of you, Frank. I'm sorry we are late."

Alice gave her father a tight hug, careful not to topple him over. "Thank you, Papa."

"Oh, my darling gel. You don't have to thank me for anything," he said, returning her embrace.

Alice gazed up at him and saw the sadness in his eyes as he looked down at her. Her father had also once worked in the mill. However, an inexperienced hand had incorrectly stacked some barrels, causing them to escape their confines, crushing his leg beyond repair. With his badly deformed leg and the crutch he required to get around, no mill was willing to offer him work—to them he was as good as useless.

It didn't matter to Alice, though, he was still her Papa and she loved him more than anybody else in the world, apart from her Mama of course, who she loved equally.

"Come, Alice," her mother said pulling her towards the enamel washbasin. "Let's get cleaned up."

Alice dutifully did as her mother asked, forcing her hands into the frigid water.

Her stomach grumbled, reminding her of how hungry she was, although there would be barely enough food, being that the family had to survive on the pittance that she and her mother earned. Times may be hard in the Smythe household, but Alice knew there was always plenty of love to go around.

CHAPTER 2

*A*lice's lunch pail slammed against her leg as she walked briskly beside her mother, the cold metal thudding against her uncovered skin causing her to wince with nearly every step. It was still dark out, the morning air crisp and cold, but clogged with the smell of the smoke pumping out of the factory chimneys, causing the fog to turn to London smog. Alice liked to draw in the soot that was left behind with her fingers, but she always received a scolding from her mother whenever she did, her mother reminding her that she had only two sets of clothes and washing them was an arduous chore, especially when they ended up nearly as dirty from being dried in the rancid atmosphere.

"Look," her mother said suddenly, pointing to the ramshackle shanty to their left. "It looks like Martha and Lincoln Peterson have moved on after all."

Sure enough, Alice saw the front door boarded up. She remembered the kindly older couple who had worked in the same mill, as most of their neighbourhood did. "What happened to them, Ma?" she asked, tugging on her hand.

Her mother's face twisted into a frown. "Lincoln was too old to pick up the cotton any longer or carry the heavy loads and Martha's back finally gave way and she could not manage the looms. I'm afraid they have no need for them in the mill now, so they have been let go. It is a disgrace to treat elderly people in such a way. They have worked their whole lives at the mill and when times get hard, they are transported off to the workhouse."

Alice's face crumpled into a grimace. Martha Peterson had always been very kind to her, sneaking Alice a few sweet treats that she had pilfered from one of the market vendors. Alice enjoyed the peppermint candies whilst she worked, they seemed to make the dreary drudge of the day go by much quicker.

"It's despicable," her mother continued, tugging Alice along. "What is to happen to us when we are unable to carry on? Will we lose our home as well? Will we starve in the gutters, waiting for someone to throw us a crumb or two?" She drew in a breath, looking down at her daughter. "Never you mind my foolish talk," she said, squeezing her daughter's hand. "We are far, far away from the gutter, my darling gel. What with your wage and mine, we will survive, eh?"

Alice nodded and they moved on, though she couldn't help but look back at the empty shanty building. Surely her parents would never let them starve, would they?

As they neared the big black factory gates, Alice and her mother fell into line with the rest of their colleagues. A line of thin, sallow-skinned, doe-eyed men, women, and children waited for their turn to make their mark in the attendance book. Alice's signature was a neatly pencilled X, where she always tried to make the lines as straight as she could. Alice had never attended school and neither had her mother and father, earning money was far more important than learning her letters. Although, when she had a moment to dream, she would wonder what it was like to read one of the large books she saw on the factory office shelf.

The first of the sun's rays were just starting to light the sky by the time Alice and her mother arrived at the front of the line, the rumble of carriage wheels across the cobblestoned street catching Alice's attention, her breath fogging in the morning air as she watched it pull up in front of the owner's townhouse property. It was situated just a short distance from where she was standing. Her mother had informed her that Mr and Mrs Langford, the mill owners, lived in the grand house with big square windows and an imposing black front door that possessed an enormous brass door knocker. Alice rarely saw anyone going in or out of the property, she was far too small to see out of the factory windows. She spied Mrs Langford standing at the top of the grey stone steps. Her gown today was a deep blue velvet, studded with little glass beads that reminded Alice of the stars in the dark indigo night skies on a clear summer's night.

The carriage door was opened by a footmen dressed in smart green livery with gold brocade, and a young boy of around twelve years old with jet black hair climbed out, racing halfway up the stairs before coming to a sudden halt, seemingly aware of Alice's eyes upon him. She watched with amazement as he turned and stared right back at her, his bright blue eyes widening as he did so.

Alice felt that she should duck her head or turn away, but she didn't, she dared to raise her hand, giving him a small friendly wave.

For a moment she didn't think he had seen the movement, but then his face split into a broad grin and he returned the gesture, much to her delight and happiness.

"Matthew!" a stern voiced called out.

They both turned at his name and Alice realised his mother was waiting for him to greet her, his once bright smile fading as he moved the rest of the way up the steps.

Alice felt her mother pull on her hand, and this time she was forced to turn away, finding the man at the entrance glaring at her. "Yer mark," he grumbled, shoving the pencil towards her.

She dutifully drew her neat X on the paper, and he waved them through the cold, dank entrance of the factory. Another day of hard toil was upon them—although Alice didn't forget about the boy who had taken a brief moment out of his day to wave pleasantly to her.

By the afternoon, he was slipping from her mind and her thoughts were on sweeping the factory floor as quickly as possible, not wanting to receive Master Turney's wrath.

She darted quickly underneath and around the noisy clacking machines, the covering over her head pulled tightly around her hair so that there were no loose strands to catch in the fast-moving machinery.

"Hello there," a bright voice sounded behind her.

Alice nearly lost her footing and tumbled over, so shocked by the softly spoken voice coming in her direction. She gulped when she recognised the boy from the carriage that morning. His clothing was not like the other factory boys, his shirt clean and starched without any patches and his smart black boots far too shiny to have walked around the factory for more than a few minutes.

"Who are you?" she blurted out rudely, grasping her besom broom in front of her body, as if it gave her some sort of protection.

He offered her a small smile. "Why, I'm Master Matthew Langford. What's your name?" he enquired, bowing elaborately.

"Miss Alice Smythe," she said giggling lightly at his showmanship, her eyes darting around in case Master Turney was watching.

Matthew looked at her broom, his face pulling into a frown. "Are you done sweeping for now?"

Alice inspected the floor beneath her feet, "Mm-hm," she nodded.

"Well, I want to play," he announced, grinning happily, his hands tucked jauntily into his trousers. "Please say you will come and play with me; I am so lonely all alone in that big house?"

"I… I shouldn't, I've got to…" Alice stammered, taking a step backward. Her mother had already warned her that the factory was no place to play, especially not when she was supposed to be sweeping and working hard.

"Don't worry we can play with your broom," Matthew said. "I'm sure your Mama won't mind."

Alice opened her mouth to tell him no, that she needed to continue with her chores, but she couldn't get the words past her lips. She did want to play so very much, though. She was tired of working all the time. Besides which, wouldn't her mother be upset if she turned down Mr Langford's son, who was demanding that she entertain him.

Hadn't her mother always instilled in her that they were to do whatever the factory owner wanted them to do, to keep their jobs? She didn't want them to lose their jobs. "If I do, you can't possibly tell my Ma or Master Turney," Alice finally agreed, hesitantly.

His expression was one of pure delight and happiness. "I won't. I swear on it!" He held out his immaculate hand for her to take. "Come. I have something I wish to show you."

Alice bravely put her broom aside and placed her small hand in his, but not before she had given it a surreptitious wipe on the back of her pinafore. His hand was far warmer and cleaner than hers. "Goodness, your fingers are icy cold, where are your gloves?" he demanded.

"I... I forgot them," she said quickly, too embarrassed to tell him that she didn't own a pair. Her mother had promised to make her some for the winter months, but with work and affording the materials, she had yet to do so.

He made a sound of exasperation before he pulled a pair of fine sheepskin mittens from his pocket, handing them to her. "Here," Matthew said, thrusting them into her free hand. "You can have mine."

Alice's breath caught as the soft suede brushed over her fingers. She had never felt something so wonderful before. "I couldn't possibly."

"You can and you will," he insisted, his jaw tightening. "If you want to play with me, you will take them."

Not wanting to defy his command, she did as he said, pulling her hand out of his to tug the gloves on, the soft fleecy lining instantly warming her skin. "There," Matthew stated, looking relieved that she had actually put them on before grabbing her hand again. "Now, we can play."

Soon Alice forgot all about her work and her mother as they ran through the big empty rooms of the upper floors of the factory. Climbing some steep rickety stairs, Matthew took her to the roof where they could gaze out over all of London. Alice swore she could see Big Ben in the distance. Her father had once told her about the time he had seen the building up close, and it had struck the hour twelve times with loud clangs. Then, pulling her back down the staircase, he guided her to a small, secret garden, accessed through an ornate wrought-iron gate.

"What do you think?" he asked, eager for her answer.

"It's beautiful," Alice gushed as she gazed around at the lush verdant patch of land. She had only ever seen trees and bushes like these once before, when her parents had taken her to the park for her last birthday, a rare treat indeed.

When her stomach rumbled, Matthew quickly went inside the house, returning with some warm jam tarts that cook had just made for him. They ate them in the garden, Alice's feet swinging from the iron bench where they sat hidden away from prying eyes.

"I wish I could do this every day," she said before licking the strawberry jam from her fingers. She sighed with sheer happiness; the tart had to be the most wonderful thing she had ever put in her mouth. Alice knew she would be dreaming of the crumbly pastry and sweetened fruit for days afterwards.

"Well, why can't you?" Matthew asked, reaching to catch his mittens before they fell to the ground and placing them in Alice's lap. "I am going to be here for a little while. We can meet every day after your mother has started her work."

Alice opened her mouth, but the sharp ringing of the bell caught her attention and her blood curdled in her veins. "Oh no!" she cried, hopping off the bench. "I must get back!" She had yet to finish her duties and if Master Turney found out she hadn't done so, she would be asked to leave her employ.

"Alice, please, wait," Matthew called after her, running close behind as Alice hurried back inside the factory, not stopping to listen to Matthew. She needed to get back as fast as she could. What on earth had possessed her to leave her work and enjoy a day's play. She was not like Matthew, she had to work, otherwise her family would go hungry.

Racing up the three flights of stairs, the staircase groaned under her incessant pounding, but it was nothing compared to the frantic beating of her heart.

Her worn boots skidded to a stop when she saw her mother standing there, her face stark white and Master Turney stood next to her, his hands firmly placed on his hips. "Alice Smythe!" he yelled, his face mottled with anger. "Where the bloody 'ell have you been all this time?"

CHAPTER 3

*A*lice wanted to run and hide, pretend that she had never left her post. The last time she had seen Master Turney this bleedin' mad, he had nearly beaten a man to death. "I... I" she stuttered, too young and naïve to form the words.

"Master Turney, please," her mother begged, tugging on the man's arm as he advanced toward Alice, slapping his hands together. "She's naught but a child! We will work for no wages as her penance."

Turney shook off her mother's grasp, grabbing roughly for Alice's arm causing her to shriek and her mother to weep. "You weren't at your post," he growled, spittle flying from his mouth, landing on her cheek. "Where were you, gel?"

Alice couldn't speak. It mattered not where she was or what she was doing. Master Turney was going to punish her regardless.

"She was with me. Now, unhand her, I tell you!" Matthew stood close by, trying as hard as he might to be the voice of authority.

Alice felt the swell of tears press into her eyes, but she refused to cry.

"Master Matthew, whatever are you doing here, in the factory?" Master Turney questioned, his eyes widening ever so slightly, but still with a vice like grip on Alice.

"Why in God's name are you treating her like this?" Matthew queried, his voice becoming less commanding by the minute but knowing that nothing good was going to happen to Alice.

"She's a factory worker, my factory worker," the man informed the master's son. "And she abandoned her post. She must be punished for it."

Alice quivered in his grasp, but she didn't dare try to fight him. It would only make her penance far worse.

"Punished?" Matthew questioned as Master Turney started to drag Alice toward one of the machines that had already stopped for the day. "But you can't. She is a young girl, younger than me."

"You there," Master Turney interrupted, looking at a fellow factory worker. "Take Master Matthew back to his parents. I am certain they are wondering where he is."

"No!" Matthew shouted as he was pulled away, leaving Alice to her fate, one that he'd had a hand in creating. Alice heard the sounds of a scuffle taking place behind her and soon enough Matthew had been removed. It was because of him that she was in this predicament. She wanted him to leave. He didn't belong here, in her world; he would never understand what it was like to be a poor factory worker.

Master Turney shoved Alice against the cold hard metal of the machinery, then turning her around abruptly, he glared at her. "Don't you dare move," he growled, his fingers digging into her thin bony shoulder.

Alice whimpered but did as he asked, knowing what was coming to her.

"Please, I'm begging you!" her mother cried from somewhere in the near distance.

Alice shut her eyes tightly as she heard the sound of the belt being pulled from Master Turney's trousers, the clang of the heavy metal buckle sending a shiver through her body.

"You must be punished, Alice Smythe, else what will the other's think. That they too can desert their posts to go off with the master's son and get up to Lord knows what?" he said, slapping the leather against his hand. "And I'm docking you a week's worth of wages for disobeying the rules."

"That's enough," her mother sobbed. "Take mine as well but please do not harm her. For pity's sake, she is only seven years old."

"Take that woman away," Master Turney snarled.

Alice took her mind away from the moment, forcing herself to think of anything else but what was coming to her. She flinched as the belt snaked through the air, making contact with her delicate young skin with a deafening thud.

ALICE WINCED as she straightened her small body, trying not to touch any area along the middle of her back lest her wounds break open again and start to bleed. The lashes from where the belt had torn through her thin muslin dress and hit her skin were just starting to heal. To aid their healing, her mother had wound a strip of moistened cloth around her torso, almost like a strait jacket, except her arms were free to carry on with her work.

She had warned Alice not to upset Master Turney again. Without her extra wages, Alice knew they would be eating less for the next week, and it was all her own fault.

Actually, it was Master Matthew's fault, and she would never forgive him. He had tricked her into doing something bad that had had her mother crying into her pillow every night since. The ache in her back meant that she could never get comfortable, and was a constant reminder of her foolishness.

When Matthew had come to find her the following day, Alice had ignored him, darting through the machines until she could no longer see him.

Today, however, he had found her as she was coming out from underneath one of the looms, her body hurt far too much to try and run from him. "Alice, please, I'm so sorry..." he started as she picked up her broom in defence. "I didn't mean for that to happen. Please believe me."

"Go away," she mumbled, furiously sweeping the cotton dregs from the floor.

"Please," he tried again. "I have brought you something."

Alice didn't want whatever Matthew Langford had got for her, not even if it was a delicious flaky jam tart. "Go away," she cried, raising her voice above the machinery.

"No," he stated, his own voice rising with irritation now. "I'm sorry, Alice. I didn't know. I couldn't stop myself. The thought of having someone to play with was so appealing and when I saw you wave at me, I simply couldn't resist." His voice cracked and she finally raised her head, seeing the hurt in his eyes. "So, what did you bring?" she whispered.

Matthew cleared his throat before reaching into his pocket, pulling out a shiny blue object. "It is a glass marble. Have you ever seen one before?"

She shook her head and he reached for her hand, his skin warm and soft against her calloused hand. She obediently opened it and he placed the object in her palm. "I tried to find one that matched mine exactly," he stated, pulling out another marble from his jacket pocket. "See?"

Alice looked from the pretty bright blue marble to the one Matthew was holding between his fingers. They looked alike and they were the colour of the summer sky on a brilliant sunny day. "Now we can pretend to play together without you getting into trouble with Turney," he said in a low voice. "All you have to do is hold it up for me to see, and then I will know that you are thinking of me?"

"Mm-hm, I can do that," she answered nodding her head softly whilst clenching the cool glass marble in her fingers. She wouldn't even show her mother that she had it. It would be their secret.

Matthew stepped back, tucking his marble back into his pocket. "I will let you get back to your work, it wouldn't do to let Master Turney know that we have been speaking."

Alice watched him go before allowing a small smile to cross her face. She had something of her own, something that no one could take away from her and Matthew had given it to her.

THE YEARS PASSED and Alice grew too big to run underneath the machines, moving to work alongside her mother. She was good at any jobs she was given, working from sunup until sundown without a word of complaint. She had well and truly learnt her lesson all those years ago, the scars still remaining across her back, and she had no desire to add to them.

Her friendship with Matthew had grown too. During his breaks from school, she would catch a glimpse of him as he moved through the factory with his father, half listening to him, and half making faces in her direction to try and get her to laugh.

Some days he could only hold up the marble before he was forced to move on, causing Alice to do the same, secretly, so that no one else saw their brief encounters. In those times, they would share a clandestine smile, something that no one else knew about. Then, she would picture herself as something more than just a mere factory worker. Maybe a shop girl with a fancy uniform or a waitress in one of the upmarket cafés.

The moments were always fleeting. Alice longed to spend more time with Matthew in the garden, like she had on that fateful day so long ago, perhaps sharing a strawberry tart or two with the factory owner's son, but she knew she never could. They were completely different people from very different walks of life; he was going to inherit the family business, she was destined to work all her days in the very same business that he owned.

Alice kept her emotional distance, no matter how close Matthew was to her, allowing herself a moment or two to enjoy their friendship before she closed off her feelings and tried to shake him from her mind, clutching the marble in her pocket as a reminder of their long-term friendship.

It was for the best, she supposed, as she grabbed the wooden spool of cotton thread and changed it for another quickly before her mother could finish. She and Matthew were on different paths for their future, Alice knew that the rest of her days would be spent here working in Matthew Langford's family firm.

Late at night, when her parents were asleep and she was huddled under the threadbare blankets covering her thin body, Alice would pull out the marble and hold it in her hand, wishing her life could be different. She had seen what working in the factory had done to the older girls and women like her mother whose bodies were ravaged by the hard work in the punishing environment, causing so many to pass before their time.

She knew she would never wear the beautiful gowns that Matthew's mother wore or ever be an equal to him. On occasion she had seen the beautiful young women who visited with their parents, fluttering their eyelashes in Matthew's direction, as if trying to catch the eye of the wealthy factory owner's son was their sole aim in life. Theirs would be a marriage to combine the family fortunes, of that she was certain.

Alice smiled to herself as she carefully tucked the marble back and pulled the blanket up tighter around her shoulders. It would do her no good to set her sights on someone such as Matthew Langford. She would likely never truly speak to him properly ever again. She simply should be satisfied that he was happy to share their small secret.

CHAPTER 4

"Matthew, are you listening?"

Matthew Langford looked away from Alice and into the angry eyes of his father. "Yes… of course I am, Father."

"I don't think so, your attention was taken with something else," his father stated, his eyes attempting to find whatever his son had been looking at. "How do you expect to manage this factory for yourself one day, if you do not pay any interest to what I have to say?"

Matthew sighed inwardly, placing the marble discreetly back into his jacket pocket. "I'm sorry, Father. I thought I saw something amiss over there, that is all."

His father cleared his throat, clasping his hands behind his back. "All of this, now you have finished school, is your legacy, Matthew. This is what will clothe you, put food on your table, find you a good wife and pay for the children you will no doubt have. It goes without saying that any potential wife will have enough wealth to combine with ours to further promote The Langford Cotton Mill Empire."

Matthew fought not to roll his eyes at the latter. He was hardly any age, and his father was already wishing that there was a suitable young woman on the horizon. He was certain that his mother had a list drawn up of prospective brides from the upper echelons of society. Matthew doubted that any woman would be interested in marrying him, after all, they would have to live next to the soot covered factory that was his father's legacy.

"Now," his father continued, "explain to me how the cotton is shipped and brought to the factory, once more, from the beginning."

Matthew drew in a deep breath biting back any retort he wished to say, before he restarted the long explanation and, by the time he and his father had walked the length of the floor, Matthew had successfully recited what his father wanted to hear.

"You have no interest, do you?" His father huffed loudly.

Before he answered, Matthew paused. He wanted to answer his father honestly. There had been a moment in his life when he would have said yes truthfully, that he had enjoyed the click clack of the machines, the fine fibres that floated through the mill atmosphere and the loose thread that accumulated in the storage rooms as a result.

That was, however, before he had witnessed Alice's punishment all those years ago. Ever since then, Matthew hadn't been able to ignore the way that the workers looked, their withdrawn, withered, and undernourished faces, or how the children didn't smile as they ran under the machines. Instead, their faces held terror and panic as they risked their young lives. It was not a place that he wanted to inherit, but if he did have to, he intended to manage the business differently. He wanted to look after his workers with compassion and benevolence. Surely, that was the only way he could make amends for how Alice had been treated all those years ago.

"It is no matter," his father continued before he found the right words. "I am sending you to The

Wetherby Cotton Mill, in Bolton, to stay with my brother, Winston, at his enterprise. Now, he will ensure that you understand that this is your legacy, Matthew. You shall stay there until Winston informs me that you have received sufficient training."

Matthew swallowed. He didn't want to go to his uncle, who he knew to be a brute. He wanted to stay here, with his family and close to Alice. "Father, I..."

His father waved a hand dismissively at him, cutting off any further complaint. "Don't say another word, I have made up my mind. You are too easily distracted here. Some time spent with Winston will give you time to learn all about what is needed to run the entire operation, since he does not have his own son and heir."

Forthwith, Matthew was sent to live with his Uncle Winston and Aunt Lucinda. He was a harsh man who didn't believe in anything but work, and hard work, too. His Aunt spent her time cowering from her bullish husband or simply hiding herself away. Matthew often pondered on the good fortune that they had never been blessed with children of their own. Matthew was certain that they would have lived a hellish life, worse than he had endured. He spent the long workdays begrudgingly growing used to the routine of rising well before the sun was above the horizon and retiring when the skies were dark. He learnt all there was to know about the business, from the orders to the manufacturing of their products, and through to the selling of their goods to the local clothing factories. The years flew by with fleeting visits to his parents and the Langford site. Each time he would search Alice out amongst the workers, clandestinely revealing their secret to each other when the opportunity arose. Even though Alice toiled hard, it did nothing to dim her resilience. When she walked through the factory hallways, heads would turn, unable to stop themselves from staring at her. Her hair, sometimes free of its constraints, was like a golden halo shimmering around her beautiful features. Matthew wanted to order the other men back to their work but knew it would do no good. He had to be patient and wait until he was able to act.

Back in Lancashire, in the evenings after supper, he would retire to his bedroom. Not only because he did not find his uncle's company appealing, but also because he wished to spend the time alone, rolling the worn marble around on his desk.

He hadn't seen Alice for some time now and he wondered if she still carried hers? Matthew wasn't certain. He hoped that she did. In his letters home, he wanted to ask of her welfare, but never dared. Sitting down at his desk, he pulled out another piece of creamy paper and picked up his pen, dipping it in the ink well carefully.

Dearest Alice, he began, biting his lower lip as the tip scratched across the paper, forming the words he had thought about all that day. *I hope this letter finds you well. The weather has turned cold here, and I must confess, I prefer the warmth of the sun on my face than the grey dismal mist that seems to never truly dissipate up here in the north of the country. How is the weather in London? I imagine it's much the same. Mama says I can come home for Christmas and I'm looking forward to seeing the factory and, most of all, you. Do you still have your marble? If not, I will give you another as the thought of you holding it in your hand, thinking of me, is all that keeps me going these days...*

Matthew sighed at the last words he had just written, wishing that he didn't sound so desperate.

Not that Alice would ever see them. Matthew knew that Alice had never been taught to read so there was no use sending her letters. He now had several tucked safely in his travel chest, hidden underneath some books. When he felt rather lonely, he would pen her another missive, pretending that she would read it and laugh or be concerned about him. He told her all he was feeling: his thoughts, his fears, his wants, even the occasional happy moments.

Yet all he did with them was carefully fold the paper and press his wax seal on the envelope, ensuring that no one else read the words meant solely for Alice. It gave Matthew hope that one day he could see her again, then he would be able to deliver the letters to her personally, to show her he had never forgotten about her.

It was strange that he had such an infatuation with a factory girl who he only saw from afar, but those moments were etched into his memory. Recently, he was unable to shake the thoughts of Alice from his mind. He wasn't sure that he could run the factory alongside his father, not if he continued to manage it in the brutal fashion that he currently did, with the vicious punishment of innocent children and the poor wages that meant families had difficulty putting food on the table. Let alone enough energy to be able to do a full day's work.

Matthew grabbed the marble and tucked it in the dish beside the bed, where he would likely touch it during the night for comfort. The letter he would put away in the morning along with the many others. Tomorrow morning, he would again awaken with the stoic face that he used whenever he was in his uncle's presence.

CHAPTER 5

*A*lice pulled her hair back tightly, securing it at the nape of her neck before putting her scarf over her head. It was something she could do in the dark, which was good considering the light was still dim outside. She didn't dare light one of the oil lanterns, not wanting to wake her ailing father and her mother, who she knew had been up in the night, her cough causing havoc through her emaciated body. At times, Alice wondered how her mother managed to carry on working, she looked as though she would pass out at the shifts end.

After pulling on her scuffed boots, Alice made her way to the sink, choosing a crust of bread leftover from yesterday's supper as her breakfast. The baker had burnt the last batch of loaves and though she had been exhausted from her long day at work, Alice had stopped to see what he had to offer at a reduced price.

To her surprise, her mother was already waiting by the front door, gripping her lunch pail tightly. "Don't forget to take this," she whispered.

"I didn't expect you to be up Mama. I was prepared to tell Master Turney that you would be in a little later."

"And have him dock me too much pay," her mother said shaking her head sorrowfully. "I would never give that man the satisfaction."

Alice dutifully took her lunch pail, and they stole out of the shanty in the darkness, barely making a sound. Others joined them on the soot covered sidewalks as they walked to the already lit factories in the distance. She stifled a yawn and kept pace with her mother, the cold biting into her threadbare coat. Her gloves, a patchwork of holes from use, did nothing to keep her fingers warm, Alice found herself shoving her hands into the pockets of her coat, her fingers brushing over the cold piece of glass she always had on her person.

Her marble, Matthew's marble.

Even her mother knew nothing of the sentimental token she had kept as a reminder of a friendship that could never be. Her thoughts of the factory owner's son were few and far between as the years had passed, but the marble always brought her back to that one moment in her young life and how he had not seen her as a dirty factory worker but perhaps a friend.

Alice and her mother walked onto the factory floor after having made their marks on the ledger. They had taken their places at the machines that Alice had come to think of as their own. For hours she removed the wooden spindles and gathered the material for her mother, even running the machine herself whenever her mother needed a brief respite.

During her own momentary break, Alice stepped outside of the factory walls to eat her meagre lunch, eating the hard, stale bread and a wafer-thin slice of cheese. Once she had finished, Alice retrieved the marble from her coat pocket and stared at the imposing townhouse that overshadowed the factory. She knew that Matthew was not there.

She didn't trouble herself too much with thoughts of him. He had likely forgotten about her and thrown his marble away.

"What do ye have there?"

Alice turned to find another girl standing nearby, her eyes on the marble that Alice was holding between her fingers. "Nothing much," Alice said quickly, tucking it back into her pocket. "In fact, nothing at all."

The girl took a step forward, her eyes gleaming. "Let me see it."

Alice recognised the girl as Bess; most folks tended to stay away from her. "No, it's mine."

"I don't care," Bess stated, reaching for Alice. "I want it."

"No," Alice said again, balling her hand into a fist. "You aren't going to get it."

Bess smiled maliciously. "Let's just see about that, shall we?"

Alice backed up but she wasn't fast enough as Bess launched at her, and they went to the ground in a flurry of skirts and fists. Having been in a factory all her life, Alice knew how to defend herself, but Bess was meaner and stronger, landing the first punch on Alice's jaw. Pain exploded through her face and Alice briefly saw stars before she started to fight back, knowing that Bess wasn't going to stop until she had retrieved the marble.

It didn't take long before one of the men noticed and Bess was pulled off Alice, still swinging her fists. "You!" the foreman barked, pointing at Alice. "Get back to your post!"

Alice scrambled off toward her mother, not wanting to give them any reason for punishing her. Once she reached the third floor of the factory, her mother's eyes widened as she took in her daughter's disheveled state. She reached for Alice, but Alice backed away, not wanting her mother to touch her. She felt dirty for what she had done.

"What happened?" her mother whispered, glancing around as if the foreman was going to say something.

"Nothing," Alice quickly replied, dabbing at her cut lip with the sleeve of her dress. "Nothing of any consequence." She didn't want to worry her mother. Neither did she want her to go to the foreman and demand that Bess be punished. Alice was old enough to take care of her own mess now.

It wasn't until they were on their way home that her mother spoke up about the incident. "Mama, it really is nothing," Alice insisted, her fingers curling tightly around the marble. "Just a bit of a disagreement, that is all."

Her mother sighed. "Alice, I don't want you to lose your job and fall victim to the streets, do you hear me? The streets are no place for a young woman such as yourself, the ruffians do nothing but take what isn't theirs and prey on the hard-working folks like us. It is no way to live."

Alice pursed her lips together, knowing it would make no difference if she told her mother that she wasn't the one to start the tussle.

"You are lucky that Master Turney wasn't here to see you," her mother continued as they shuffled down the dark street, the lamplighters yet to light the gas lamps. "You know what he would have done."

Alice shuddered inwardly at the thought. She knew exactly what Turney would have done, and what his punishments consisted of. The scars on her back were proof enough that he didn't care whether the penalty was dealt to a child or not. She had faced the wrath of his belt and it was something that she had no desire to experience again.

Her mother tucked her arm in Alice's. "Keep your head down, Alice, my girl. We don't want you to lose your position at the factory. There is little left in terms of earning any money unless you are on your back."

"I understand." Alice swallowed, keeping her eyes straight ahead so that her mother couldn't see the tears that glimmered in her eyes. Her mother was right. She couldn't lose this position. There was no other work that would pay close to the wage they were making at the factory. "I won't cause any more trouble. I promise."

Her mother laid her head on Alice's shoulder as they walked. "Good girl. I know your life should be more, but this is the best I can do, Alice. I swear it."

Alice thought about the townhouse she had gazed at earlier, and the way she had defended herself against Bess. Her mother was right. It was the best life she could have in the East End of London.

Her mother straightened, clearing her throat. "Come, Papa will be wondering where we are."

CHAPTER 6

THREE MONTHS LATER...

*A*lice darted through the throng of carts, carriages and people clogging the street, knowing exactly where to step so that she wouldn't lose her footing on the uneven, slick cobblestones. Sunday was her only day off from the factory but instead of recuperating from her long weeks work, she spent the time earning a little extra money.

Alice quickly sidestepped an oncoming carriage, and barely avoiding being trampled by the horse's hooves, she resumed her pace, anxiously glancing up at the darkening sky. There was a threat of rain in the air and Alice knew that her time was limited today, she had been up early at dawn, making her rounds and gathering the coins that now jingled in the pouch hidden deep within her skirts.

Finding the small brick home on the fringe of the East End, Alice knocked politely on the side door, stepping back to wait for someone to answer. When they did, it was a dour faced cook, her apron stretching wide across her portly frame. "No handouts," she barked, moving to close the door.

"No, wait," Alice stated, wedging her booted foot into the doorway before the woman could shut it completely. "I have a delivery for Mrs Harston."

The cook eyed the bundle that Alice held out. "You're the seamstress."

Alice nodded. "Aye. This is the gown she wanted altered."

Some of the distrust left the cook's face and she opened the door wider. "You might as well come in before you get soaking wet. I will fetch the money she gave me to give to you."

Alice's scuffed boots clip clopped noisily into a tidy kitchen, the smell of roasting beef making her stomach growl loudly. She didn't dare touch anything, not wanting to give the woman any reason to not use her services again. The gown was perhaps the loveliest fabric she had ever seen and why Mrs Harston had allowed Alice to take it to her shanty, she wasn't certain, but she had made sure there wasn't a speck of dust on it.

The cook returned a moment later and took the bundle, handing Alice the coins. "Here. Mrs Harston said to come back next week."

"Thank you," Alice replied, clutching the coins. As her stomach growled loudly again, the cook frowned, placing the dress on the counter. "Sit, girl. You look as if you haven't had a decent meal in weeks."

More like months, she thought. "But I can't possibly..."

The cook waved a hand at her. "I'm telling you to sit. Mrs Harston wouldn't like it that you walked out of her home hungry."

Seeing no other choice, Alice gathered her skirts and sat on the chair whilst the cook busied herself with a plate. She didn't want to take the charity, but having a good, hot meal inside of her was too much to turn down these days. Ever since her mother had died last month, after finally succumbing to her bad chest, Alice had barely been able to scrape together enough food for two people to live off.

Her father was inconsolable most days, consumed by the grief of losing his true love. Alice had grieved too, but the day after they had put her mother in the ground, just outside of London town, she had gone back to work at the factory. After all, there was no other choice if they were to survive the harsh realities of their lives.

It had only taken a week or two to figure out that her wage wasn't going to be enough to sustain them. One of the other women at the factory had taken pity on her and introduced her to a local seamstress who needed additional help and after a week of watching her, Alice was taking work home to complete by candlelight after her shift at the factory had finished.

Unlike the factory, the quicker that Alice could complete the work, the more money she could earn, and no matter how stiff her fingers were from the incessant needle pricking, Alice didn't waste any time in completing her work.

"Here," the cook announced, sliding a plate full of beef and mashed potatoes towards Alice. "Eat quickly and I will pack you something to take back home with you."

Tears crowded Alice's eyes. "I... I don't know what to say."

"Eat it and say nothing," the cook replied, moving away so that Alice could eat in peace.

Alice ate her fill gratefully and then took the small bundle wrapped in an old cloth from the kindly older woman. It contained still warm bread from the oven and a couple of slices of the roasted beef. She had tried to pay her for it, but the cook just waved her out of the door. Now, her father would have something fresh to eat as well.

Before she could return home Alice still had more work to complete. She tucked the loaf into the canvas bag slung over her shoulder and headed to the rundown inn near the docks, careful to stick to the shadows of the late morning so that she wouldn't be noticed. The owner of the inn was what her mother would have called 'a lady of the night'. Miss Eliza Jenkins was waiting for Alice on the front step, a cigarette hanging out of her rouged painted lips.

"Ah, there you are. I almost gave up on you."

"I'm sorry, I was waylaid," Alice said in a rushed breath. "Where are they?"

Miss Jenkins nodded her head inside and Alice followed her in, the faded wallpaper and stale smell of ale and smoke no longer bothering her. In fact, Eliza Jenkins had offered her a position at the inn when they had first met, stating she would go for a pretty price with her young, youthful face. Alice had shuddered, turning her kind offer down in an instant, but she kept her wits about her and had asked if there was anything else she could help with.

Laundry, it seemed, was something very important to Miss Jenkins. While the inn looked as if it were crumbling down around her ears, she prided herself on having clean sheets for her clients every day instead of once a week like many others in the same line of work. Alice came by on Sundays to wash them in the back room, scrubbing them until they were as white as she could make them with the harsh lye soap.

"We've been busy this week," Eliza Jenkins said by way of an apology as Alice gazed at the pile of sheets awaiting her. "Do it quickly and I will double your wage today."

Alice straightened her shoulders and stepped into the room. She would do it quicker than Eliza Jenkins could ever imagine.

HOURS LATER, Alice stepped out of the inn, her hands red raw from the harsh soap and constant scrubbing. True to her word, Eliza Jenkins had doubled her wage and now Alice had enough money to pay the rent and purchase some extra food.

It had been a good day, even if she was exhausted and her body aching from the hard manual work.

"You don't look like one of Eliza's girls."

Alice looked up to find a youth lounging against the side of the building, playing with a piece of straw between his lips, a strand of bright red hair falling over his forehead.

"What did you say?"

He nodded toward the inn. "Miss Eliza Jenkins. You don't look like the rest of her workers. Is she trying to draw in a different sort of clientele these days?"

"I'm not one of her girls," Alice remarked tartly.

He launched himself off the wall and stepped in front of her, and she fought the urge to push him down and run. It would only draw attention, and considering she was still at the docks, the last thing she needed was to draw notice to herself else she might not make it home to her father. His green eyes drifted down over her body.

"Aye, you aren't. Yer far too skinny to be of Eliza's working girls."

Alice gasped, affronted. "The same could be said of you, too scrawny by far," she fired back, taking in his tall lanky form.

His eyes widened and she could tell she had surprised him. "Well, now," he said, finally, sticking out his hand. "I'm Declan."

"I'm not interested," she replied, brushing past him.

"How do you know I was going to offer you anything?" he called out after her.

Alice turned, smirking. "Whatever it is, I'm not interested." He looked to be the sort of trouble her mother had warned her about months ago, one that would have her floating in the Thames by the end of the week.

Declan grinned. "You're right. I do want something but it's not what you think. How would you like to not work yourself to the bone, but still make plenty of money for you and your family?"

"It is not possible," Alice said slowly. The only kind of work that existed like that took place in the building behind them and she wasn't interested in selling her body, not for any amount of money.

"Oh, it is possible," Declan replied, shoving his hands deep into the pockets of his muddy brown trousers. "It's not without risk, but I could use someone like you. You know, clever and smart."

Alice shook her head. "I'm still not interested," she replied before walking away at a fast pace. Declan didn't call her back nor did she look behind her again, knowing that it was far too improper to delve into something that was more than likely illegal.

She had too much that depended on her, including her father, to take such a risk.

CHAPTER 7

"*L*et me help ye with that, my darling gel."

Alice gave her father a small smile as she lugged the heavy pot from the fire. "Don't worry, I can manage, Papa. Please go and sit. I will have supper ready shortly."

"You are just like yer Ma," he muttered to himself as he hobbled over to the small wooden table, his crude crutch clanking against the earthen floor. "Never thinking I can help you out."

"That's not what I think at all," Alice admonished as she ladled the thin stew into the chipped bowl. "You have been up since I have been home. It is time for you to rest now."

Her father continued to grumble as she cut a slice of the fresh bread. She had been able to trade it for a mending job the previous day. She scraped a small amount of lard over it. She knew that he wished to do more, to show that he wasn't as useless as everyone else saw him as. Her father had been trying hard since her mother had passed to procure work, but everyone saw him using a crutch and assumed he wouldn't be able to do anything of any use.

Carrying the soup bowls and bread to the small rickety table, she placed one in front of her father. "Eat, Papa," she urged. "Before it grows cold."

He dipped his spoon in the watery stew and Alice waited until he took his first bite before she did the same, trying not to look too eager in eating her own bowlful. She had forgone supper last night so that he could have an extra portion, telling him that she wasn't hungry.

Truthfully, Alice was sometimes too tired to even pick up a spoon. Between her work at the factory and her odd jobs, sewing and washing laundry, there wasn't much energy or time for anything else. Often, Alice would come home in the evening and simply collapse onto her bed. She tried to maintain a smile for her father, though inside she wasn't sure how much longer she could keep going at her present rate—she was exhausted.

Of course, he wished for her to meet a good, honest man and have a family of her own. At her age, most of the girls had done just that, though they still stayed on at the factory, working to help pay the rent and put food on the table, but there was no way that she could leave her father.

After supper, Alice's father waved her away when she tried to wash the dishes. "I've got it," he mumbled, dipping his hands into the cold water. "It is the least I can do. Now, you be off to bed with you. You look dead on your feet."

Alice gave him a grateful smile, stripping down behind the curtain that her father had strung up for her and throwing on her threadbare nightgown, shivering as the cold air snuck through the cracks of their shanty wall. It didn't take long for her to burrow herself under the covers, her body shaking until she was able to garner a little warmth.

She could hear her father on the other side of the curtain, washing and drying their dishes, his crutch making the softest thudding sound on the floor.

That was when the tears would come. She had grown very good at muffling her sobs, not wanting to upset her father. If only her mother were still alive; they wouldn't be rich, but she wouldn't have to work quite so hard.

She wasn't though, and now it was just the two of them. Alice had to be stronger than she had ever thought possible.

She had to ensure that her father continued to have food on the table and a roof over his head. It was all up to her.

JUST A FEW DAYS LATER, Alice was moving through the swarm of people crowding in the street, holding her sparse coat close to her body. The weather had turned icy cold once more, crushing any thoughts of an early spring. The air was thick with soot from the chimneys overhead and Alice had to cover her nose on more than one occasion as she passed the ramshackle buildings, glad to have finally delivered her last sewing parcel of the early evening. She was returning home and would have to scrounge up a dinner for them, their supplies beginning to run low.

The laundry work had ceased over the past month as Eliza Jenkins had been taken ill suddenly, and all she had now was her sewing work to bring in the extra money.

In the absence of her additional income, it meant less food in their cupboards and Alice didn't have any idea of what she was going to do if Eliza Jenkins didn't return to her rather distasteful work.

"Ho! You!"

Alice slowed her steps as she saw a familiar figure jogging toward her. She had seen Declan on and off many times since their first encounter near the docks, but she had stayed well away from him.

Of course, like Alice, time had caught up with his gangly frame and now he possessed a wide set of shoulders under his thick overcoat, his head bare despite the biting wind which caused his still fiery red hair to blow across his freckled face. His jaw was dusted with the same red hair and Alice supposed he could be described as handsome, with the perennial straw stuck between his cherry red lips.

"What do you want now?" she bit out.

He drew up short at her side, matching her step as she started to walk once more.

"Hey, now, whatever did I do to you to deserve that? I'm a friendly sort, you know."

Alice glanced over at him. "I'm sure you remember us meeting before?"

He scratched his head. "No, I think I would remember such a pretty face. Yer not one of Eliza Jenkins's girls, are you?" he said, grinning widely.

Alice's cheeks burned. "What? Of course not!"

Declan shrugged his shoulders. "Didn't think so."

"What do you want this time?" she enquired, wanting to shoo him from her side. "I have some very important business I need to be getting on with."

"Oh, wait!" Declan announced. "I do remember you! We met at the docks, a while ago now." This time he winked cheekily at her.

Alice stopped on the sidewalk, her hands on her hips as she faced the handsome boy.

"And I ignored you then, as I am inclined to now."

His bold smile sent her heart fluttering, as probably many a girl's had before, when he had bestowed it upon them. "I have something I think you will be interested in," Declan replied, glancing at Alice's hand. "No husband?"

Alice tucked her hands into her coat pockets. "It is no concern of yours. I bid you good day."

"Wait," Declan called out, touching her arm gently. "You look like a strong woman. I've need of that. How would you like to make a bit more money?"

"No, not if I'm right in what you are thinking!" Alice responded, affronted that he would even suggest such a thing.

Declan rolled his eyes. "Not like that!" Tucking her arm in his, he steered Alice to the nearest bakery, strolling in as if he owned the business. "Come, let me fill your pockets with delicious treats to take back home."

After he had selected a large quantity of baked goods to be packaged, Declan passed her perhaps the largest scone she had ever seen. Her stomach rumbled at the heavenly scent as Alice tried to think of the last time, she'd had one. "Go on," Declan encouraged, his expression moving to something akin to sympathy as he passed over the money to the eager baker behind the counter. "Eat."

Alice did, the sweet treat dissolving on her tongue. She wanted to savour the taste, but she was too hungry for that.

"In good faith," he answered, handing her the brown paper parcel she would take home to her father, "if you will simply sit and listen to what I have to say."

Alice chewed on her lower lip. She had seen the amount of money that Declan had handed over without flinching at the price. She wanted to live like that, to not have to work so hard to get so little. "Alright, I will listen, but I am not promising anything."

He gave her a toothy smile as he extended his arm. "Of course not."

Alice allowed Declan to lead her to a nearby bench. "I run a smuggling operation for my boss," he murmured in a low voice. "When the cargo ships come in at the docks, nobody really checks who unloads the cargo, they just accept that it is done, and if some of those goods happen to come my way, well, so be it."

"But that's stealing," Alice said in a hushed tone, her eyes darting around to see who was in the vicinity.

Declan's grin returned. "Nah, it is only stealing if you get caught. We burn the leftover crates, so no one knows. When you think of all that cargo coming in, what we take is a tiny amount in comparison, so no one notices." He looked at her reddened hands. "It's a hell of a lot easier than what you're currently doing."

He was right about that. Alice was working herself to the bone trying to provide enough food for herself and her father as well as paying the rent on the shanty. How much longer could she carry on?

"Think about it," Declan said as he stood up, tucking his thumbs into the small pockets of his waistcoat. "Come and find me at the docks tomorrow night if you're interested. You can tag along, see that there's not much to it." His eyes flickered over her dress. "Wear men's clothing. You will attract too much attention looking like that. The dock workers cannot be trusted when there is a pretty woman in their midst."

Before Alice could reply, he was gone, disappearing into the crowd of people hurrying home.

Swallowing, she glanced down at the parcel in her lap, full of treats that her father was likely going to have questions about. Despite how easy and harmless Declan made it sound, Alice knew that it was still stealing.

But what was the problem? The businessmen who owned the cargo were extremely wealthy, well beyond her imagination. Surely, they wouldn't miss a few items, would they? She knew her mother would have been disappointed with her, but she needed to earn the extra money if she was going to be able to support her father.

Pushing off from the bench, Alice blended into the crowd, clutching the parcel to her chest. She would think on what Declan was offering, nothing more… for now.

CHAPTER 8

SIX MONTHS LATER…

*A*lice hefted the wooden crate and moved swiftly down the gangway, careful not to trip over her own feet in the process. It had been drizzling on and off all day and the boards were slick, which made the trek even more perilous.

Not only that, but her arms were aching from all the crates that she had transferred from the boat to the warehouse over the last three hours and if she had to carry another one, Alice was certain she would drop it right into the murky water of the River Thames.

Once her boots were clear of the planks, Alice hurried to the warehouse, her eyes keenly attuned to the darkness surrounding her. "That took long enough," Declan hissed as he took the wooden pallet from her. "Is this the last one?"

"Yes," Alice breathed in relief, slumping against the wall. "That's it for tonight."

Declan moved to the pile that had accumulated in the middle of the room, placing the crate on top.

"Then shut the door so we can get to work."

Alice forced her feet to move to the heavy warehouse door, pushing it closed and throwing the latch. Already the other runners, some of them children half her age, were working on the piles of crates scattered throughout the warehouse, their crowbars and hammers falling into a steady rhythm as they tore apart the crates once the wares were removed.

They ranged from exotic spices and fine silks to products waiting to be manufactured. They would be carefully bundled into hessian sacks and transported to another warehouse, where the boss would take a look and dole out the earnings to Declan, who would in turn give the runners their cut.

That included Alice.

She turned back to her own stack of crates, reaching for the small hammer and crowbar hidden in her coat. It had taken her some time to get used to wearing breeches, her hair pushed tightly under a flat cap and her breasts bound to keep her chest as flat as possible. Her delicate features did pose a problem as she had learnt to keep her head down and not to speak unless absolutely necessary.

That way there were no questions.

Declan was already starting to remove the goods from her crate, likely knowing that she wouldn't be able to finish it all by herself. After spending much of the daylight hours toiling away in the factory, Alice had very little strength left, but if she wanted her money, she had hurry up and demolish the crates and sort out the goods within.

Alice moved to the first one, striking it with her hammer and splintering the wood. The first time she had unloaded the cargo, she had been terrified, but there had been a thrill tingling up her spine when she realised how much money she had earned for one night's work. She had been able to stock the cupboards with food for the rest of the week.

For that alone, she had felt the risk was worth it.

Alice couldn't give up her position at the factory. While Declan's operation was very fruitful, a tiny voice in her head wouldn't let her forget that it was illegal and if she needed to, she could stop the cargo work and return to what she had been doing.

Every time she thought about telling Declan that she was finished, Alice remembered the look on her father's face when he knew she had more than enough money to pay the rent, or to put food on their plates.

Besides, even though she was particularly drained this night, it was still better than having to do her other extra jobs to make ends meet. A cargo boat didn't dock every evening, meaning that sometimes Alice was able to spend a little time catching up on her lost sleep.

She made three times as much cash working for Declan and his boss than she ever had laundering Eliza Jenkin's sheets or sewing fiddly hems for the fine ladies who supped tea in the afternoons.

"Quickly now," Declan urged, breaking Alice out of her thoughts. "We don't have all night."

Neither did Alice. It was less than two hours until she would have to start work at the factory.

Somehow, even with her tired arms, Alice managed to break down all her crates, adding them to the pile where later they would be burnt to ashes, hiding any evidence of their unlawful trade. Declan made sure his boss received the goods by the following morning, although the man held onto them for a week or two before passing them on to his unsuspecting clients.

Alice didn't ask any questions beyond what Declan wanted to tell her, and she didn't want to know either. It was best that she knew as little as possible.

The less she knew the better.

After the warehouse floor was swept, eliminating any remaining crate detritus, Declan let them all go, promising payment within a matter of days. "Good work," he grunted, opening the door. "Fancy a pint with me?" he asked Alice.

He often requested her company, and Alice turned him down each time. While Declan was a handsome young man, she wanted nothing to do with him beyond their business arrangement. "I'm sorry but I need to be at the factory in half an hour," Alice said apologetically. "Perhaps another time."

"When are you going to stop all that and come work for me full time, Alice?" he asked softly as she passed through the door. "There's a spot for you here, you know. It's right at my side."

Alice didn't respond, hurrying into the dark before he could stop her. The draw to work with Declan full time pulled on her relentlessly, yet she held back. Right now, she could walk away, go back to her old life, and not think another thing about it.

If she was to work only for him, then her livelihood and that of her father's would rest solely upon Declan's ability to keep them out of prison.

Alice wasn't ready to make such a leap of faith, not yet.

Hurrying through the deserted streets of London, Alice pulled out the old token of friendship and luck she had kept for such a long, long while. The marble went with her on every run, not because she felt it would be stolen, but more for good luck, ensuring that she came to no harm.

The sun was starting to crest by the time she reached the East End again, dodging the carts and carriages already out and about, despite the early morning hour. Her stomach rumbled but Alice ignored it, desperate to get to the factory. Once there, she would pull out the bundle of clothing she had stashed in the courtyard and change out of the breeches so that there would be no questions about her odd choice of clothing. Inside that bundle was a small piece of bread and hard cheese that would be her breakfast and lunch too.

If her father noticed her missing from her bed at night, he said nothing. Often, Alice wondered if he thought she had a beau that she was sneaking out to meet with.

At least that was what she told herself and would be what she told him if he ever asked.

Clutching the hard marble tightly in her grasp, Alice finally saw the brick façade of the factory, framed by the impending sunrise, and smiled tiredly. She could get through this day and there wouldn't be any more runs for at least two more nights.

She was overdue for some rest, at least her body and mind were.

Alice forced herself to put one foot in front of the other, closing the distance between herself and the factory. She was almost there.

She was so focused on getting to the factory on time that Alice didn't see that she was crossing the cobblestone street until it was too late, hearing the whicker of the horse bearing down upon her.

Startled, she looked up in time to see the whites of the horses' eyes, frozen in fear as she waited to be trampled under the heavy hooves.

"Get out of the way, you stupid girl!" A gruff voice sounded.

Alice drew in a tortured breath. She hadn't been run over at all, the carriage stopping just in the nick of time.

The marble in her pocket had given her luck again, keeping her safe from harm. Alice moved to rub her thumb over the worn trinket and gasped as she realised it wasn't there. "No," she cried out, looking frantically around the street. She couldn't lose it, not now!

Heedless of the coach driver yelling at her, Alice dropped to her knees, her hands searching the grubby cobblestones. He would have to go around her because she wasn't going to leave this spot until she found the treasured item.

CHAPTER 9

Matthew watched as the familiar town of London came into view, tapping his fingers on his thigh nervously. While he knew that he would eventually come home, he hadn't anticipated it would be earlier than expected. He and his uncle had found common ground and were able to work amicably together, his uncle willing to listen to Matthew's ideas on how to manage the factory in a more compassionate manner, agreeing that if the workers were healthier then it would show in their productivity.

When the summons had come, Matthew hadn't been sure that he had believed the news. After all, his father had always seemed invincible, a formidable man who would live a long and active life.

Unfortunately, it was apparent he couldn't, for his father had now passed and the fate of their family's legacy lay squarely on his shoulders.

His uncle had informed him he was more than ready to take on such an important responsibility, having worked with Matthew and seen his abilities grow, admiring his tenacity. He had garnered all the knowledge required to run the London side of the business. Now they had finally been able to agree on a common ground and together they had worked on new strategies that Matthew had been expecting to present to his father, but now it mattered not. He was able to introduce the plans without having to convince his bullish father of their worth.

Shifting on the leather seat, Matthew reached into the pocket of his waistcoat and pulled out the familiar marble, rubbing his fingers over the cool glass. He'd always known that he would come home eventually.

It was what he had been groomed for, wasn't it? Yet Matthew's stomach twisted in knots every time he thought about his future.

Was he sure this was what he wanted?

Clearing his throat, Matthew shook his head, forcing the dark thoughts from his mind. It was what he was destined for. He could set in motion any of his ideas for the factory. He had free rein to run the factory as he chose to, and he intended to do so.

That was what he had always wanted, to change the way the people of the East End worked.

His father would never have agreed to any of his plans. Matthew was certain of that fact.

Matthew could still hardly believe that Nicholas Langford's funeral was upon them. Matthew knew that if his father were still alive, he would have told his only son to quit dragging his feet and return home immediately.

What made the whole situation worse for the family, his mother especially, was that his father had died in the arms of his mistress, sullying their family name. Though it had come as no surprise to anyone that his father was involved with another woman, it still produced salacious gossip.

It didn't matter anymore. Matthew had dutifully come home to bury his father and become the next Langford in line to own and run the factory, but this time it would be run the way he wanted, not by the tactics his father had commandeered.

The coach turned down the familiar cobblestone street and the air suddenly turned thick with the all too familiar smell of soot, causing Matthew to wrinkle his nose. He had grown used to spending his free time on the moors where the air was fresh and clean. Living in the East End there seemed to be no quick way out of town, as there had been in the north of England.

He could see recognisable buildings through either side of the carriage windows, meaning he was nearly home. Tucking the marble away carefully, Matthew ran a hand through his dark hair and clenched his jaw tightly. Once the coach stopped, he would be expected to look and act like a gentleman, ready to step into his father's footsteps. Gone was the carefree young man who had left his uncle's property mere days ago. There would be no more racing across the wild moorland or spending his free time penning letters to a recipient who would likely never see them.

No, he had to be a different person once he arrived.

The coach jolted suddenly, and Matthew was nearly thrown to the floor, hearing the drivers shout of alarm. Once he righted himself, Matthew threw open the door, climbing down the small set of steps. "What's going on?" he asked the driver.

"Some fool urchin ran right out in front of me!" the driver cried out, pointing to a scruffily dressed body in front of the horse.

"I have to find it!"

Matthew froze. It couldn't be. The voice was older but still familiar to his ears, a voice that had haunted him for so many years.

Hurrying to where the person was scrabbling in the dirt, he gazed down to see a mass of blonde hair, the woman searching in the cobblestones for some unknown object, heedless of the coach or the stamping of the horses' hooves near her own small hands. He couldn't see her face, but the rapid beat of his heart didn't need to see her.

He *knew* that voice.

"Git on with you, gel!" the driver shouted, moving to step down from the coach to forcibly remove her himself.

"I will take care of this," Matthew said immediately, holding up his hand.

The driver's eyes widened but he ducked his head, finding his seat once more, and Matthew moved to the woman quickly, spying what she was looking for almost immediately. "Is this what you are trying to find?" he asked softly, picking up the familiar object.

She looked up and Matthew's breath caught as he peered into her clear blue eyes, framed by a perfectly heart shaped face. "You found it! Thank goodness you found it!" she replied happily, snatching it out of his hands.

Matthew waited for her to acknowledge him, but she didn't, tucking it back into the pocket of a worn coat instead. Did she not realise who he was?

Did she not remember him?

"Alice?"

Alice looked up; her eyes wary as she took a few steps back. "Yes?"

It was her. Matthew's tongue was suddenly too thick for his mouth, but he forced himself to straighten, clearing his throat. "It is me. Matthew. Matthew Langford."

He watched as her eyes wandered over his face, taking in the fine cut of his clothing that he had hastily thrown on in the dark of this morning. "Matthew?"

"It's Alice, right?" he responded, pulling out the marble from his own pocket.

A small smile broke out over her lovely features and Matthew was transfixed as she pulled the marble back out, holding up the identical children's toy.

"You're home."

"Mm-hm, my father has passed," he replied, clenching the marble in his fist. "I have been called back home to take over the running of the factory."

Alice's mouth worked before settling in a thin line. "I heard of his death. I'm sorry for your loss."

He wondered if she really meant what she was saying, after the way she had been treated. "Are you still working at the factory?"

"Oh, goodness!" Alice said, her eyes rounding. "I have to go. Else I will be late! It was so good to see you."

"Wait!" he called out after her, but she was already moving into the crush of people clogging the street, disappearing from his sight.

Matthew continued to watch the space, long after she had vanished.

It was Alice and she was all grown up. She was no longer the impish child that had entertained the bored factory owner's son all those years ago, but a woman, a beautiful woman with a life that Matthew had no idea what it consisted of.

"Mr Langford?"

Shaking himself out of his thoughts, he looked up at the waiting driver. "My apologies," he murmured, moving back to the carriage and climbing in. The vehicle moved forward immediately as Matthew leant back against the crisp leather seat. She had seemed happy to see him, hadn't she? It had been only a brief moment when they had acknowledged one another. So quick, he had not been able to decipher whether she wore a band on her wedding finger or not, but he had noticed that her clothing was still threadbare and near enough rags. She had dirty smudges on her cheeks with dark grey circles under her eyes and she had looked tired, very tired indeed.

When he replayed her image through his mind, he wondered whether she had been wearing breeches? Surely not. In that fact, he must have been mistaken, he had never seen her wear trousers before.

A small smile flashed across Matthew's face. He had seen Alice. Had she thought of him often? Perhaps not as frequently as he had about her, but at least she had remembered who he was.

One thing was for certain, he hadn't expected her to be quite so beautiful…

CHAPTER 10

The workday flew past despite how exhausted Alice was, mainly because she kept looking for a tall, handsome gentleman to come striding across the factory floor at any moment.

Matthew Langford was back, and she could hardly believe that she had seen him face to face.

When she had looked up and found him holding out her marble, she couldn't have been more delighted. She had been far too stunned to react properly. He had grown, as she had, but he was far more handsome than she ever could have imagined. His hair had darkened with age and his sharp jawline only served to accentuate his features. His body had lost the lankiness of youth and was now broad with a sturdy musculature. He wore good clothing with a fine cut. The gentleman's perennial accessory, a gold pocket watch, was tucked neatly into his smart waistcoat. One thing was certain, Matthew Langford had grown into a very striking young man.

Now he was here and despite the years that had separated them, Alice's heart had fluttered at the sight.

Of course, she had heard, like the rest of the factory workers, of Nicholas Langford's untimely death.

In the arms of his mistress, no less. Alice thought about how Matthew must be feeling. She had been so busy between the runs with Declan and making certain she didn't miss her days in the factory, that she hadn't had that much time to dwell on his feelings.

For some odd reason the thought of Matthew returning home hadn't crossed her mind until she had seen him this morning. It was to be expected, of course, although the prodigal son had been gone for some time, only returning to the family home for special occasions and festivities. Alice secretly thought that she may never see him up close ever again.

Apparently, fate had other plans.

When her workday finally ended, Alice hurried to the market to find some food for supper, banishing any thoughts of Matthew Langford away for now. It didn't really matter that he was back. It wasn't as if they were going to be together anymore. He was going to take over as factory owner, and she would be nothing more than a lowly worker in the factory that he now owned.

Alice just hoped that he didn't have the same brutish nature that his father had displayed with the workers. She couldn't imagine that he would have. He had been so very good to her all those years ago.

After choosing a day-old loaf of bread and a few root vegetables, Alice made her way to the shanty town just as the sun was setting behind the wooden, soot covered buildings. There was also no good reason why she would see any more of Matthew. She lived here and he lived in the large mansion next to the factory with his mother. They were on two opposite ends of London society and now that he had come home, Alice knew it wouldn't be too much longer before he took a wife, one in keeping with his station in society. She would bring him the prestige he needed to move through the society circles, garnering extra business.

Drawing in a breath, Alice shook her head. She shouldn't waste her thoughts on Matthew Langford. No, all she needed to think about was a good supper and her bed, glad that there was no cargo run tonight.

It was hard to keep up with what she needed to do as it was.

Pushing open the rickety door to the shanty, Alice stepped in. "Papa, I'm sorry I'm late..."

Her words died in her throat as she found her father seated at the table, next to him a familiar face that had haunted her all day long. "Wh... what are you doing here?"

"Miss Smythe," Matthew acknowledged with a dip of his head. "I was just telling your father that you should be home by now. The workday finished a little while ago."

"I had to go to the market, for some food," she said, showing her paltry rations to the men before shutting the door behind her. "Is there something amiss?" What if Matthew had come to sack her in front of her father? Though he had no reason to do so, she was good at her work.

"How did you find us?" she asked sharply, worry creeping into her chest. "Why are you here?"

"Alice," her father said crisply, disappointment written on his face. "That is no way to talk to your employer. I apologise, Mr Langford, for my daughter's apparent lack of good manners."

"Please, call me Matthew whilst you are in your own home," he said displaying a soft smile. "And there's no need to apologise. Alice has every right to question my intentions here."

Alice forced herself to move to the small kitchen area, placing her wares from the market on the wood stove. Suddenly her home, the small shanty that she shared with her father, seemed to pale in comparison to the massive home that Matthew was used to. Her cheeks heated as she thought about the dirt that likely covered the floor, dirt that she should have cleaned up weeks ago but hadn't had the time.

Or the soot that coated the walls from the wood stove and fireplace, with no maids to sweep it down so that it wouldn't continue to gather.

She was… well, embarrassed that he should see her home like this.

"I confess," Matthew was saying, "that I asked one of the other factory workers where you lived, after seeing you today. I wanted to apologise for not taking the time to properly greet you."

Alice snorted. "I was the one hurrying off, if you remember," she replied, turning around to face him. "If anything, it should be me apologising to you."

He gave her a small smile. "I do confess, I have ulterior motives for being here. I have been discussing a certain business arrangement with your father here."

Alice eyed him warily. It was easy to think of Matthew as a stranger, given the way he looked and the years that had passed between them. She really didn't trust anyone these days.

"He wants to give me a position at the factory," her father added.

"What?" What position could her father hold in the factory with his disability?

"There are requirements, of course," Matthew stated. "He needs to learn his sums and his letters."

Alice's breath caught. She had always wished to learn how to read and write, detesting the fact that she couldn't read the crates that Declan constantly had them break up or even sign her name carefully on the roster each morning at the factory. "I... I don't understand."

"Your father has given his life and that of his family's to my family's company," Matthew said softly. "Or rather my company, now. I wish to repay your family's loyalty, something that my own father should have done many years ago."

Tears burned in Alice's eyes, but she refused to shed them. There had to be something more that Matthew wanted. "Tomorrow evening," he finished. "I will start the lessons tomorrow evening."

"That is a grand idea," her father responded. "Don't you agree, Alice?"

There was nothing for her to disagree with. Matthew was offering her father a godsend, one that she had prayed for.

He was offering him something to believe in again. "Yes. I think it is a grand idea."

"Then I will be off and leave you to your evening," Matthew replied, standing. The gentlemen shook hands and Alice followed Matthew to the door, stepping out into the cold night air. "Why are you doing this for us?" she asked the moment she pulled the door to.

Matthew arched a brow. "I am doing nothing. I am simply offering him a position of employment, which will be of benefit to me."

Alice crossed her arms over her chest, glaring at him. "You want something from us, don't you?"

"Of course not," he replied, looking affronted that she would even suggest that was the reason he was trying to help them. "I want to help you, Alice." Matthew clasped his hands behind his back. "I was very sorry to hear of your mother's passing. Your father was telling me that she died some time ago from the scourge of all mill workers, it would seem."

Alice swallowed the grief threatening to bubble up within her. "I don't expect you even remember her."

A sad smile crossed his face. "Oh, but I do, actually. She was a hard worker and always had a kind word for me whenever I made the rounds with my father at the factory." He stepped back, giving her a polite bow. "I will see you as soon as my father's funeral has been completed, Alice."

"Wait," she called after him, causing Matthew to turn. "You do know I can't pay you."

"I don't expect you to," he answered immediately. "It is merely a business decision, Alice, and please, I would like for you to accompany your father as well. It will do you well in the future, if you could also read and write."

Alice let Matthew walk away then, biting her lower lip as she watched him disappear down the darkened street. Was it too much to hope that he was going to follow through with his plans and not disappoint her father tomorrow evening?

With a sigh, she moved back into the building, the room somewhat dimmer since Matthew had departed. If he didn't return, she wouldn't blame him. It was hard to be in a dismal place such as this when he was used to the finer things in life…

CHAPTER 11

"We therefore commit this body to the ground, earth to earth, ashes to ashes, dust to dust; in sure and certain hope of the Resurrection to eternal life."

Matthew fought the urge to fidget as he watched the dirt drift from the priest's hand and land with a thud onto the wooden casket in the ground below. Beside him, his mother cried softly into her handkerchief, her hand clutching his arm tightly with every word the priest spoke.

There were murmurs of amens and signs of the cross before the man of the cloth stepped back, the mourners already starting to make their way back to the warm bricks inside their coaches. Matthew barely knew the attendees, most of them old friends of his father, and he doubted that any of them cared for the fool either.

He had hardly shed a tear for his father, that was for certain. With the wisdom of age, he could see what sort of a man he was... a loathsome, adulterous bully.

Finally, his mother squeezed his arm and he helped her back to the warmth of the carriage, tucking a blanket around her slight body. "That was a nice service," she remarked as Matthew sat across from her, rubbing his gloved hands together briskly.

"Aye," he replied, the coach jerking into motion. "I wish you would have allowed me to shut down the factory today."

His mother turned her face toward the glass window. "Your father wouldn't have heard of it. The work still needs to continue, Matthew."

While he agreed with the statement, it didn't mean that one day would ruin them financially. He wanted to give the workers a chance to mourn if they wished to, though he knew there were few who would. "Of course," he murmured.

"I see you don't agree with me." She sighed. "And it's your factory now for you to do as you wish, Matthew, but there are certain protocols that we must follow. There can't be allowances."

"I understand," he said, clenching his jaw. His mother thought the same way that his father had, and it bothered him more than it should.

The wake had been a sombre affair, the mourners seeming to be more interested in the salacious gossip regarding his father's untimely death than actually grieving his passing. Fortunately, his mother had been ignorant to the guest's mutterings, something that Matthew was eternally grateful for.

Now, it was just the two of them, seated together at either end of the long dining room table, with the silence of the house all around them. "Tell me," his mother enquired, after the tea was poured, "what are your plans for the future, Matthew?"

"I plan on sorting out the factory," he stated plainly. "And finding out what the true state of the company affairs are."

"And maybe a wife?" his mother questioned hesitantly.

"A what?" Matthew spluttered.

His mother picked up her cup, blowing on it carefully. "A wife, Matthew. You will be expected to find one quickly, now that you are the owner of the Langford Cotton Mill. I can arrange a dinner party and invite some eligible young ladies."

Matthew dropped his napkin, pushing his chair back. "Don't you think it's a bit too early to be thinking of such a thing, Mama?"

She didn't flinch at his harsh tone, taking a small sip of her tea before responding. "You will see, Matthew, that it's the next course of action. I know you don't like the idea, but someone has to take care of you. Businesses in London are not going to take you seriously without a wife and a family."

Matthew stood, glaring at his mother. The last thing he wanted was a society wife to dangle on his arm. "Please excuse me while I go and see to the business that may fail without the support of a fine wife."

"Please, Matthew, don't be angry with me," his mother said quietly as he moved toward the door. "I'm only looking after your interests in the best way I can."

He didn't reply, exiting the room before he said something that he would regret.

AFTER A TRYING day poring over the financial statements and ledger books, Matthew made his way to the shanty town, pulling his coat tighter around his shoulders. He had traded the fine suit he had worn earlier in the day for a pair of rough work trousers and a worn coat from one of the stable hands, wanting to fit in with his unfamiliar surroundings. Matthew knew his mother would be annoyed if she knew where he was going.

Turning down a familiar alleyway, Matthew kept his head down as he passed clusters of rough looking men, hoping that he blended in. He had tried hard to emulate the worn factory workers look and, so far, no one seemed any the wiser of his origins.

Matthew pondered on what he had achieved since his father's demise. He had rounded up the scoundrels, such as the likes of Master Turney, and asked them to leave his employ immediately. He had given them a good severance pay which had stopped their grumblings. Although more than likely the money wouldn't reach their front doors. No, likely it would be spent at the nearest tavern.

In their place he had appointed men who he could trust to treat the workers fairly. He had a feeling that once his mother found out what he had done, she would be appalled.

Matthew didn't care, it was his factory now and he could do with it as he saw fit, and he would. He needed to be able to trust the people working for him, to ensure the safety and health of his employees.

Reaching the door to Alice's home, Matthew hesitated before knocking. When he had come to this place earlier, he had been shocked and appalled to see how Alice lived with her father. The shanty was little more than a wooden shack, hardly fit for animals to live in, much less a human being. Soot covered every surface in this area from the chimneys over his head to the cobblestone streets below his feet.

His heart lurched when he saw the drawn looks of those that he passed, the weariness set in their faces.

Matthew wondered whether there was more he could do, but he needed to start with Alice and her father first.

Secretly he knew it was more than just improving their wellbeing that had him standing in front of the door. It was Alice that brought him to the grimy streets of the East End.

Drawing in a breath, he rapped on the door with his knuckles. It opened almost immediately, the aroma of cooking heavy in the air. Alice stood in the doorway, her hair tumbling down around her shoulders. She looked surprised. "You came?" she questioned.

"Didn't I tell you I would?" he answered, clearing his throat.

Alice swallowed before she stepped aside. "Then, please, come in."

Matthew wiped the dirt from his shoes, surprised to find the shanty a little cleaner than it had been the last time. "I have some stew leftover," Alice was saying, moving to the pot. "If you would like some?"

"Please," he replied as he removed his coat and gloves, placing them on the peg hammered into the wall.

"I wish I had some ale to serve you," her father said, gesturing for Matthew to take a seat at the small table. "Or whiskey."

Matthew grinned, reaching deep into his pocket and removing a silver flask he had placed there earlier. He pushed it across the table. "Why don't I share some of this with you instead?"

Alice's father smiled, appreciating the gesture, and Matthew understood that it had been worth taking the few precious moments to fill the flask, vowing to bring more on his next trip.

Alice sat the dented tin bowl in front of him, the steam wafted up into his face and he gave her a warm smile as he accepted a spoon. The stew was lacking some of the tastiness that he was used to, but it was hearty and warm, and he finished it all. "Thank you," he said appreciating the food that was no doubt sparse in this household.

She gave him a tight smile as she collected his empty bowl and Matthew pulled the slate and chalk from his satchel. "Are you ready?"

Alice shook her head, untying the apron around her slender waist. "I cannot stay. I have, err, errands to attend to tonight. Maybe next time."

Matthew frowned. "It is nightfall." What sort of errands could she possibly have to attend to at night?

But she didn't reply, instead kissing her father's cheek softly. "I will see you later, Papa."

"Be careful, my gel," her father replied, worry creasing his face.

Alice glanced quickly at Matthew before she was gone, tucking her scarf around her neck. "She has another job," her father said once the door was shut. "At the docks."

Matthew felt the first frisson of fear. The only job he knew that existed at the docks was one that he hoped Alice hadn't fallen into.

"I don't know much about it," her father continued, rubbing his chin thoughtfully. "But if I can learn my letters, then hopefully my girl won't have to work so much, or so hard."

That was why he was here. "Well, then, we best get started."

The older man nodded, and Matthew laid the slate on the table, though his thoughts were on Alice for the better part of the next hour. She hadn't returned by the time he had finished for the evening and after saying good night, Matthew changed his direction toward the docks, a grim look on his face. After winding through a few streets, he finally spied Alice in an alley, before ducking behind a corner, hiding himself from view. What was she doing? His stomach twisted as he watched her, staying in the shadows so Alice wouldn't see him.

He could see from his vantage point that she was now wearing a scruffy pair of trousers, puzzling him even further. The doxies liked to wear sordid dresses to attract their customers.

Alice seemed to have put on more clothing, as if she were trying to be something she wasn't… a boy.

It wasn't long before he spotted a tall man approaching her and after a brief conversation, she tucked her hand in his and they moved down the alley, away from where Matthew stood.

What was Alice involved in? Was that her lover he had just seen? Matthew's jaw worked angrily. Alice had grown into a lovely young woman, one who would turn more than a few heads whenever she walked by.

Matthew ran a hand through his hair, wanting to pull it out by its roots. His heart was pounding, what had Alice got mixed up with? Whatever it was he needed to save her from any harm.

CHAPTER 12

*A*lice's hands moved quickly as she removed the full spool and replaced it with an empty one before the rack could move toward her, breathing a sigh of relief when it didn't stop the massive machine. She was so tired, having completed a run in the small hours of the morning and stumbling to her bed with scarcely an hour or so to sleep.

That, and she had forgotten her lunch pail. It was still hanging on the peg by the door and now she was looking at a long day with only a dipper full of water as her only sustenance.

A harsh day indeed.

Placing the full spool in the barrel beside her, Alice grabbed another, thinking back to all the times she had watched her mother do the same work, remembering how she would daydream about another place and another time, far away from the constant daily grind of factory work.

Alice often did the same, wondering about faraway lands that the cargo, that she helped to steal, was imported from. Today, however, instead of another place, she couldn't help but think of another person.

Matthew, to be precise.

A sigh escaped her lips. As much as she had wished to stay yesterday evening and be tutored by Matthew with her father. She had to accompany Declan at the docks, a large cargo ship had come in and they needed to pilfer the goods before morning. Matthew's handsome face had plagued her all evening and into the early morning hours. Had he given her a second thought, or had he dismissed any thoughts of her, the moment she had left?

As if he could read her thoughts, Alice spied Matthew in the near distance, talking to his newly appointed foreman. Her cheeks flushed far more than they should have in the hot humid atmosphere.

Alice approved of the men he had chosen; they had demonstrated in the past to be good, hard honest workers, who cared about others. They were far better than Master Turney and his fellow bullies.

Alice felt the nerves in her stomach start to flutter as Matthew and the foreman made their way to her machine. Matthew was attracting the attention of the women on the factory floor, but when his eyes found hers, he looked at no one else. "Miss Smythe," he said, pausing.

"Mr Langford," she murmured. "What can I do for you?"

His eyes seemed to hold words that Alice knew he wasn't going to say and for some reason, her heart started to thud a little faster. Gone was the young boy who had given her the marble, and in his place, was the man who had become the owner of her place of work.

His eyes flickered over toward the growing spindles. "Well done, Miss Smythe, everything appears to be in order."

"Thank you, Mr Langford," she answered, giving him a polite nod.

He did the same and Alice could have sworn she saw a hint of a smile before he moved on, his hands clasped behind his back.

As she walked out into the small courtyard to take her nonexistent lunch, she found herself face to face with the new factory owner. "Alice," he said warmly. "I was hoping that you would venture out here."

"Mr Langford," she replied evenly. "I'm taking my break, if that is agreeable to you."

His eyes looked at her empty hands, a frown creasing his brow. "Surely your break should consist of some nourishment?"

"Unfortunately, I left it behind this morning," she admitted, embarrassed at her own foolishness.

"Well, then," Matthew said, holding out a small tin pail. "You can share mine."

Alice shook her head. "Oh no, I couldn't possibly."

"I insist," he said gently, holding out his arm. "I will not have my employees go hungry. Please accompany me."

Alice wanted to say no, to walk away, but she found it hard to do so.

"Please say yes, Alice," he interrupted, a teasing glint in his eye. "Or I might have to take back my marble."

"That's not possible," she murmured as she slipped her arm in his. "It was given to me a long time ago by a special friend, so it is rightfully mine."

"That is so," Matthew replied, grinning as he led her away from the courtyard and through the iron gate to his own family's garden. There they found the very same bench that they had sat on so long ago. Matthew placed the pail between them, pulling out cold beef sandwiches and offering them to Alice. It was a lovely meal, much better than the one she would have brought from home, and she wasted no time in savouring the tasty food, her stomach grumbling happily with each bite.

"Thank you," she said between bites. "It has been a long time since I have eaten a lunch so delicious and filling."

"There is plenty," Matthew stated. "I will have cook make you some sandwiches tomorrow."

Alice's good nature faded. "I don't need it, thank you." The last thing she needed was for the other workers to see that Matthew was favouring her. It was hard enough to keep them from bothering her, especially the men, without them seeing that he was giving her special treatment.

Matthew frowned. "I hope you aren't offended by the way I am treating you. I want to spend time with you, that is all."

She stared at him. "But why?" she asked. "Why are you wanting to, what is your reasoning?" Teaching her father to read and now this. She didn't understand. "We are no longer children, Matthew."

"No, it is true we are not," he responded, reaching over to take her hand.

The moment their bare skin touched, Alice shivered, feeling her own blood rush through her veins. He looked so earnest, and she wanted to lean into his touch. "Matthew," she murmured.

"We aren't children," he repeated, his thumb brushing over her knuckles lightly. "But I'm hoping that we can be something more."

Alice's lips parted, her heart hammering against her chest wall. More? What could he possibly want with her? She wasn't the sort of girl that he should even be sitting in this lovely garden with! "But, Matthew."

"Tell me that you would like the same," he said suddenly, his hand clutching hers. Alice forced herself to meet his gaze, seeing something akin to hope in his eyes. He truly could take her breath away. "I won't force you," he continued, oblivious to her thoughts, "but Alice, there is something between us, isn't there?"

Didn't he realise that she wasn't the same as him? "Matthew," she started, at a loss as to how to let him down gently. She didn't want to, enjoying the way his hand was touching hers. What would it be like to have him hold her, embrace her, kiss her?

Maybe even love her?

"Please," he urged. "Give me a chance, Alice. Give me a chance to prove myself to you."

"What could you possibly have to prove to me?" she blurted out. "You are wonderful already and I am..."

His smile grew. "I'm wonderful?"

Her cheeks flamed. "Yes, you can't imagine how that small round glass marble got me through some of the most difficult times in my life. It reminded me that at times there are others who truly care. It gave me the courage to stand up for myself when I felt that my life couldn't continue."

"I know what you are saying," he said softly. "During our time apart, I wrote you hundreds of letters."

"You did?" she asked, surprised.

He nodded. "And I want you to be able to read them, Alice. To show you that I never forgot about you."

Her heart raced. "And I want to read them too," she admitted, her mind whirling with all that was being said.

Without warning, the garden gate opened. Hearing startled gasps, they both turned to find Matthew's mother with a gaggle of young women. "Mother," Matthew said his voice sounding alarmed as he removed his hand from hers.

"Matthew," his mother replied, but her eyes were firmly on Alice. "Whatever is going on here?"

Alice stood abruptly, curtsying to his mother. Her face was aflame, but more so because of the cloying looks the prettily dressed women were giving Matthew. These were the women he should be consorting with, not her.

"Good day, Mr Langford," she forced out. She should never have allowed herself to accompany Matthew into the garden. Pretending that they were equals and the same young people from the past.

"Miss Smythe…" he started, but Alice was already through the gate, hurrying back towards the factory. He thought that they could still have the same friendship as before or maybe something else, but he was wrong. She was nothing like him or his mother.

When she finally made it back to her loom, Alice let herself draw in a breath. The tears would come later, when she was alone, when no one could hear her. Self-consciously she reached into her pocket and touched the cool glass of the marble, finding her actions foolish.

She would avoid Matthew Langford at all costs from now on, showing him that there was a clear line between the two of them. She worked for him, and he paid her wages, nothing else.

No matter how much it hurt. They didn't belong together…

CHAPTER 13

*A*lice stepped out of the shadows of the building as Declan approached, his cap pulled low, hiding his face. She had been waiting for more than an hour for him to turn up, her hands and feet numb from the freezing cold. "Where have you been?" she hissed.

Declan ignored her, glancing around at their surroundings. "Have you seen any of the boys?"

Alice shook her head. "They haven't come." It was customary for the working boys to place themselves along the street ahead and for Alice to go and check before Declan arrived. Tonight, however, she hadn't seen hide nor hair of anyone, save the constable that had been walking the beat.

"Bloody hell," Declan muttered, hunching his shoulders against the wind. "Not sure what's happened, maybe they got held up, but it looks like it's just you and me tonight then, lass."

Alice's lips parted. "We can't do this alone!" With the hired boys, they pulled thirty or forty crates from the docks and even with their additional help, her arms ached from all the hard work.

Declan took a step forward, his eyes flashing. "We will and we can. If we get just one crate, it is more than we walked in with." His voice was cold, and a shiver raced down Alice's spine. She had never had a reason to be frightened of him before, but there was something different about him tonight, he was more on edge than usual.

"Perhaps the law is onto us," she answered, trying to keep the tremor from her voice. "They have likely scared off the boys." Alice hadn't heard anything on the streets about the missing cargo, which seemed to be odd considering the amount of goods they were managing to filch. Surely someone had caught onto their lark by now.

"Hush yer trap," Declan growled. "The law are idiots, the entire lot of them! This plan is foolproof, or else

I wouldn't be running it. Got it?"

"Alright, I will do whatever it takes." Alice didn't believe that anything was foolproof, only that luck had been on their side for this long, but she wasn't about to argue with Declan. She only wished to finish the job and get back home, where she could forget about her nefarious ways.

Declan gave her a sharp nod. "Good, that's what I like to hear, Alice. You and me, we are going to bring in more money than we have ever seen before." His lips curled into a smile, and he winked at her. "Just you and me, lass."

"You and me," she repeated, hiding her sudden fear behind a smile herself. She was certain that he would abandon her if the law was onto them, but what could she do? Right now, she needed the money.

"I will go scout the dock then," Declan replied. "Wait here."

Alice watched as he disappeared into the shadows before she allowed herself to take a breath, wanting nothing more than to run in the opposite direction. Normally their runs didn't bother her so much, but not having the additional help of the others, coupled with Declan's demeanour, had her wary.

Swallowing hard, Alice forced herself to think of other things, such as Matthew's visits to her home. He came by regularly and her father's knowledge was increasing on a daily basis. He wanted the job that Matthew had offered so very much. Alice had tried and failed miserably to ignore him, especially when her father insisted that she join them. Alice hadn't wanted to, but the lure of learning how to read and write was too much for her and under Matthew's careful tutelage, Alice had already learnt her letters.

Matthew had lavished praise upon them both, and she had basked in it. When Matthew was in her home, all thoughts of who he truly was and the differences between them melted away. It was easy to think of him as one of them, especially in the clothing that he preferred during their visits. Often Alice found herself admiring his profile, only to blush when he turned his lovely eyes on her, seemingly doing the same.

It was as if that recent day in the garden had never happened, but it was futile and pointless for Alice to think that anything could become of their friendship There could never be anything more. She prided herself far too highly to be a paramour for him and he was destined to marry a high-born, well-bred lady.

Alice rested against the rough brick of the building behind her, anxiously awaiting Declan's return. Once she had learnt enough to secure another position, Alice was going to cut her ties with Declan. She had been far too lucky to not be in prison already and she wanted to keep it that way.

Besides, if her father continued to do well with his studies, they wouldn't need the additional funds she made from helping to steal the cargo. They would have another way to take care of themselves, one that was legal.

It wasn't long before Declan made an appearance again. "The coast is clear now," he murmured, motioning for Alice to follow him. "Let's get to work."

Her heart thudded in her throat as Alice followed closely behind Declan to the docks, where the ships bobbed in the dark water. A heavy fog had descended over London, giving them a little more cover so that their features would be hard to distinguish should anyone see them.

Declan motioned to the first ship and Alice drew in a breath as she moved up the rickety gangplank, where the crates were located. No one bothered to stop her as she lifted the first one and started back down the plank, careful not to fall and cause a commotion.

Over and over, she picked up the crates under the cover of the darkening fog, her arms starting to ache from the weight. Alice was glad to see that Declan was helping as well, his tower of crates stacking higher than hers could ever be.

When the floor of the ship was empty and they were back at the warehouse, Alice rested against the stack of crates, catching her breath. "Good job," Declan stated as he admired her work. "I knew you could do it."

"What do we do now?" Alice asked, straightening her cap to keep her hair underneath. Normally she would aid the boys in breaking down the crates or help Declan run the goods, but since there was only the two of them, she didn't know what to expect.

"You break down the crates," Declan ordered as he used a crowbar to open the first one under the shielded lantern light. "I will deliver the goods."

Alice picked up her hammer and waited for Declan to hand over the first crate, smashing it carefully so that she would have less splinters to clean up later.

Once she had a sizeable pile, Alice picked up the pieces and carried them out of the warehouse, placing them in the waiting wagon that Declan would take away later, since they couldn't burn the crates quick enough during the night.

A lit fire in the distance caught her eye and Alice realised that there was a group of young children standing around it, the dying flames being blown about in the wind. By the looks of their clothing, they looked worse off than Alice was, likely orphans with no home to go to.

She wished she had some extra money to give them, but she had nothing on her person to offer.

Except... Alice looked down at the broken pieces of crate in her arms, more than enough to keep the children warm until morning.

It was the least that she could do. All Declan was going to do was burn the crates anyway. He wouldn't miss a few pieces.

Alice marched over to the group. "Here," she said, shoving the broken crates towards the nearest child. "Take this, it will burn well and keep you warm for the night."

The child, who looked to be a young girl under the layer of dirt, grabbed at the wood until there was nothing left in Alice's arms. "Wot do ye want for it?" she asked haughtily. "Cos, I got nothin',"

"Well, that's good then, because I don't want anything," Alice replied softly, giving her a firm smile. "It is yours, for free."

The girl snorted and turned her back on Alice. "Nothin' is for free around 'ere."

"This is and I will leave another pile in the alleyway," she said as she turned to go. "Just in case."

Alice moved away, her shoulders feeling a little lighter as she moved back to her task. At least something good would come out of what they had done tonight, and if she could keep those children warm, then she would sleep easier.

When Declan returned, Alice had the wagon loaded with the rest of the crates, her entire body aching.

"You want a ride?" he asked, placing his hand on her shoulder. "I don't mind taking you home."

"Nah," Alice answered, not wanting Declan to see where she lived. She preferred to keep this part of her life separate from the other. "I will be fine."

Declan nodded, reaching out to brush her cheek with his finger. "You are truly one of a kind," he said gently, his eyes softening.

Yet another side of Declan she had never experienced before.

"This will not be my life forever," he continued, dropping his hand. "But I hope you will remain with me until then."

Alice wasn't certain she understood what he was saying. "I-I guess we will see," she finally forced out, stepping out of his reach. "Goodnight, Declan."

He gave her a jaunty bow. "And to you, my formidable thief."

She quickly hurried away; her emotions conflicted with what had just happened. First Matthew and now Declan appeared to have their hearts set on her...

CHAPTER 14

M atthew frowned as he carefully added up the column once more, scratching the number on the ledger before him. "Tom, do you know why we didn't receive all the goods we ordered from the last shipment?" he said, glancing at the man to his right.

Thomas Nelly, his new clerk, gave him a single nod. "I will have an answer for you before the end of the day."

Matthew leant back in his chair, tapping his pen against his hand. "I will not stand by and allow other businesses to take advantage of me simply because I am not my father."

"Understood," Tom replied. "I will see that we have answers soon enough."

Matthew returned to the ledger as the other man departed from his office, the hum of the machinery in the distance a soothing sound. If the looms were running, then he was making money to continue to run the factory and pay his workers.

Already, he had upped their wages and given them an extra day off a month, something that was almost unheard of amongst the other factories. Now they had more time to spend with their families. Matthew had worked with Tom toward organising a shift rota so that the factory was never silent, even with the additional day off.

His mother didn't understand, of course, why Matthew had thought to do something so rash—in her opinion—but Matthew knew that if their workers were loyal, they would be happier to complete their day's tasks. Whereas his father had put all his time and effort in ensuring that the product was complete, Matthew would rather spend his time investing in the people who made the product.

It was unorthodox and if it didn't work in his favour, Matthew stood to lose thousands of pounds, but it was a risk he was prepared to take.

Now, his mother was pressing him to find a wife. The other evening, soon after he had returned from the Smythe's, his mother had presented him with a stack of invitations that she was waiting to accept on his behalf to various balls and dinner parties. They were all from the wealthier families in London; although not royalty, they were good enough to elevate his station.

Matthew didn't care about his status, nor did he care to wed a simpering miss who would only want him because he had a little wealth and standing.

He wanted a different life, but he was certain his mother wouldn't understand if he told her the truth.

Spying the blue marble on his desk glinting in the unseasonably late sunshine, Matthew picked it up with a little smile on his face. The previous evening Alice had been much more open than usual. They had joked together as he listened to her read from one of his old schoolbooks. She was truly excelling in her lessons and Matthew knew that eventually he would give her his letters so that she could see how much he had valued their rather odd friendship.

How much he cared for her. It mattered not that she was from the East End. Although it would matter far more to his mother. But not to Matthew, Alice was more genuine than anyone else he had ever encountered within his own social circles.

Unfortunately, there was the small matter of the gentleman he had seen her with. Alice never once mentioned him and if her father knew about their relationship, he was certainly staying silent about it.

Did Alice care for the young man? Matthew shifted in his chair, tamping down the jealousy that threatened to rise. He wouldn't get in the middle of their relationship if she did. He would be a friend to her for as long as she wished, but he wanted to know if he still had a chance to win her favour.

"Mr Langford?"

Matthew looked up to see one of the men that oversaw the shipments of cotton clutching a piece of paper in his hand. "Yes, Tom?"

"I thought you would want to see this," Tom replied, placing the paper on his desk. "This report was brought to me by the constable. It seems someone has been breaking up the crates, your crates, as he recognised the Langford Mill mark."

Matthew brushed his hand over the symbol that every cotton crate was stamped with, feeling his anger rise. He had reported some thefts to the constabulary just this morning, with numerous crates of cotton suddenly disappearing from the cargo hold and never making it to the factory. The constable had informed him that he would investigate the theft, and it seemed that he had actually found something. "And the cotton? Where is it?"

"Nowhere to be found." Tom sighed. "It is a good thing that you cut back on production, Mr Langford. We will not have enough supplies."

Matthew slammed his hand onto the desk, making Tom jolt. "Get me the constable. I would like to speak to him."

"Yes, sir," Tom said before turning and rushing out the door.

Matthew clenched his jaw tightly as he stared down at the piece of wood from the dismantled crate. He detested a thief. A thief had no honour regarding what he was taking or how it would impact others. The cotton was imported from the colonies, from a plantation that his grandfather had established many years ago, and the crates that it was shipped in were very unique, stamped with the Langford family crest. Just one crate held a tidy profit for whoever had taken it, the cotton within likely being sold to his competitors for their use and profits.

Putting the piece of wood aside for now, Matthew turned his attention back to the ledger, assessing quickly how much he had lost from the stolen shipment. If the dock master couldn't oversee his own cargo, then Matthew would do it himself and hopefully catch whomever the thief was in the process.

The rest of the day dragged on slowly and by the time Matthew made it back home, the sky was already darkening.

"Matthew?"

Pausing on the stairs, Matthew turned at the sound of his mother's voice. She was standing at the top of the staircase, her hand on the railing and he could see that she was dressed in a deep mauve satin gown and wearing her finest jewels for the evening. "Yes, Mama."

"I'm off to the theatre," she replied, her eyes on his disheveled waistcoat. "I was hoping you might attend with me."

It was the last thing he wanted to do. "I'm sorry, Mama, there has been a situation at the docks," he answered. "I must head there straightway." It wasn't completely a lie. He did plan to go to the docks this evening and personally oversee the shipment being delivered to the factory.

But first, he was going to spend the evening at the Smythe's.

"What sort of situation?" she asked, her hand at her throat.

"Nothing for you to be concerned with," he said gently. "I will see you at breakfast tomorrow morning. Please enjoy your evening."

His mother's gaze narrowed, and he waited for her to object but she eventually just nodded, walking down the stairs and to the front door. He thought about calling her back but turned himself, making his way to his room. His mother would understand, wouldn't she? Their livelihood came first surely, but what she wouldn't understand was his growing feelings for Alice.

Matthew quickly changed, heading out of the townhouse in time to see Alice walking ahead of him, her long blonde braid swinging with the motion. Matthew jogged up to her side, some of the tension from the day's events ebbing away. "Alice."

"Matthew," she replied, giving him a quick glance. "What are you doing?"

"Walking with you," he replied, tucking his hands in his pockets. "You are getting home late tonight. I trust the owner didn't make you work later than intended."

That statement earned him a smile. "No," she said softly. "He is a good gaffer to work for."

Matthew felt himself grin. "That's good. He appears to be a sound fellow then."

They turned a corner and Alice stopped, looking towards him. Matthew drew in a breath as her eyes searched his, something soft crossing her face. "I think he is," she said. "Though I wonder why he is intrigued by a lowly factory worker."

Closing the distance between them, Matthew reached out and brushed a wayward strand of hair from her face, his fingers skimming her cheek lightly. "Because she took pity on a lonely little boy once and he fell for her right there and then."

Her lips parted and Matthew had the strongest urge to kiss her. It wouldn't be proper out on the street like this. "The question is," he continued, his eyes searching hers. "Does she feel anything for that lonely little boy?" There, he had confessed what his intentions were. It would be up to Alice to reciprocate his feelings or reject them.

Alice stared at him for a long moment. "We can't," she replied, a hitch in her voice.

"Why?" he demanded.

She was the first to look away. "I am from the East End, and you are… not."

CHAPTER 15

"And what is this one?"

Alice looked towards where Matthew was pointing, squinting at the letters. "I-t, it" she said proudly.

"That's good," Matthew replied, a grin covering his face. Alice returned his look with a smile of her own. After their tense conversation in the street and her telling him that they could not be, Matthew had been unfailingly polite. She wished he would say something, anything, about what she had said, but he hadn't spoken the entire time he had escorted her home.

What if she was wrong? What if he didn't care about her status or his own? Surely, he did. No man in his position was going to wed a woman who was just beginning to learn to read and write, a woman who hardly knew anything about the society he mixed with or how to be a wife to someone of his standing.

Her stomach twisted and she turned back to the book, the words blurring in front of her. She didn't want to think about the alternative. One day Matthew would be forced to take a wife to ensure that there was an heir to his fortune.

"Alice?"

Realising that she had been lost in her thoughts, Alice cleared her throat. "I'm sorry, I was daydreaming."

During the rest of the lesson, she concentrated on her work, working through numerous pages of the children's book before Matthew said that it was time to finish.

"Thank you," her father stated, slapping Matthew on the back. He too had worked through the book with relative ease, a broad smile on his face the entire time, proud of what he was finally achieving.

"It has been a pleasure to teach you. You are both eager students," Matthew said as Alice opened the door. "You are doing so well, Mr Smythe." Then he turned to Alice. "And you, as well."

Despite her earlier concerns, she blushed. "Thank you."

"I will see you tomorrow then," he replied, doffing his cap. "Goodnight."

"Goodnight," she murmured, forcing herself to close the door after him.

"That boy is smitten with you, Alice," her father stated, gathering the few books Matthew had left for them to practice on.

"Papa, no," Alice admonished. "You shouldn't say that."

"What?" her father asked, arching a brow. "I cannot say something that I can see with my own eyes?" He clicked his tongue as Alice started to gather her belongings for the night run, it was to be a little later tonight, so she would have to work quickly if she was to get to work on time the next morning. "Alice, my dear girl, don't let your origins dictate where you travel in life."

Alice's shoulders trembled as her father enveloped her in an embrace. "I want you to be happy, lass," he murmured. "And it matters not that you aren't part of his world. The look he gives you, I don't think he cares either."

Her father's words stayed with her as she kissed his weathered cheek. "I will think about what you have said, Papa."

"Be careful, lass," he said gravely, eyeing her as she tucked her long hair underneath the woollen cap.

"I will," she promised him before stealing into the night, her coat tails flapping behind her. She didn't want to hope, but there it was, buried in her heart—that what her father had seen might be the truth.

That Matthew had feelings for her. Given the words they had shared earlier in the evening, she knew that it was possible.

Oh, how she wanted to throw caution to the wind and tell him that she too felt the same, but there was the matter of what his mother and his peers would think if they did further their friendship into something more.

One thing was for certain though, Alice didn't want to ruin Matthew's future.

Her heart was heavy as she made her way to the dockside. Declan and a just few boys were already there, milling around. "There you are," Declan exclaimed as she drew near. "I was concerned you wouldn't come tonight."

"Why wouldn't I?" Alice questioned. "I always come, don't I?"

"Aye, you do." Declan grinned, throwing his arm around her shoulders. "Well, then. Let's get started. You go on to the first ship. I will have one of the lads join you presently." When Alice started to move away from him, he held onto her shoulders, forcing her to look at him. "I wish to talk to you about something when we have finished tonight," he said, his voice low. "Please tell me that you will allow me to do so."

He seemed so earnest that Alice was surprised. "Yes, we can talk," she said quickly.

Declan gave her a grin before releasing her. "Good. This is going to be a good night, Alice. I can feel it in my bones."

Alice didn't feel the same. There was something niggling in the back of her mind, something that told her this might not be one of her best nights. Was it because of her discussion with Matthew or was there something else bothering her?

Did Declan want to discuss their future? How would she answer him?

She couldn't possibly think of a future with him. While he had given her an opportunity to provide for her father, she didn't feel the same way about him as she did about Matthew. Her father was right. She needed to understand what Matthew's intentions were.

Alice pushed all her thoughts of Matthew and Declan aside as she made her way to the first ship, adjusting her stride so that it would be more like that of a young man's. This would be her last run, she had decided. The money she earned, while good, wasn't going to be necessary for them once her father took the position that Matthew was offering.

Walking carefully, she made it up the gangplank and reached for the first crate.

"Alice?"

A snort escaped her as she straightened at the sound. How foolish was she? She was hearing Matthew's voice all around her.

As she turned, Alice realised that it wasn't her mind playing games with her at all. Matthew was coming toward her, out of the dense fog, his eyes wide with amazement.

No, no this couldn't be happening!

Whirling around, she made a move to flee, but her hat brushed against a low hanging rigging rope, and she felt it fall from her head, her long blonde hair tumbling down.

"Hey, what is this?" a loud voice demanded from behind her. "A gel?"

She had been found out!

"Alice, don't move," Matthew called out as she hurried down the gangplank, frantic to find a way out. She didn't want him to know that she had been stealing the goods.

Shouts went up around her as her feet hit solid ground, Alice saw the other lads scattering in the distance, there was no sign of Declan. When she had started working for him, he had warned her that if anyone found out what they were doing, then it was every person for themselves and now she had to get as far away as possible.

Alice took off toward the alleyways that would lead back to the East End, knowing that if she could get to the shadows, she could lose them. It mattered not that Matthew recognised her. Surely, he wouldn't bring the constable to her home.

Lost in her worry, Alice made the wrong turn and found herself up against a high wooden fence, far too tall for her to climb.

No!

"Hey, you over there! Stop, I tell you!"

Alice turned to see the constable running down the alleyway, with Matthew right behind him. She looked back at the fence, but there was no way she could escape.

She was truly done for. Her father's face flashed before her eyes and she knew that once he found out about what she had been doing to earn the extra money that had fed them for months, he would be disappointed that she had resorted to such foolish acts.

She didn't ever want to disappoint him, but now it seemed she may well have done just that.

The constable's face was red with exertion as he reached her, grabbing her arm. "Look here, missy, you are under arrest."

Alice didn't have the energy to fight him, tears starting to burn in her eyes. She had done this. She had done the crime and whatever punishment that was decided for her would be warranted.

"Stop, constable!"

Matthew's voice pierced through the air. Alice hung her head, refusing to even meet his gaze. She couldn't. She was far too ashamed that he was here tonight, watching her steal what wasn't hers. He would think differently about her now, wouldn't he? She was nothing but a common gutter urchin.

CHAPTER 16

$\mathcal{M}$atthew had never imagined that it would be Alice involved in the thievery. How could she be the one who was stealing from him?

His Alice. No, it couldn't be true, yet here she was, her eyes wide and her expression frightened as the constable dragged her out of the alley. He was certain she would be charged with robbery and sent to prison without much of a trial.

"You!" the constable demanded, swinging his lantern toward Matthew. "Get along before I arrest you as well!"

Matthew clenched his jaw. It was his fault that Alice had been caught and he wasn't about to idly stand by and watch her be taken in. "I am Mr Matthew Langford," he forced out, drawing to his full height. "I demand you let go of my associate."

The constable arched a brow, his eyes moving over Matthew's worn clothing. "And I'm the King of England," he snorted, roughly pulling Alice. "Is this yer sweetheart then?"

"You are making a grave error, my good fellow," he tried again. He had nothing on him to prove that he was who he said he was, he couldn't blame the constable for not seeing it. "Go on, take us both in. You will see that you have arrested the owner of Langford Cotton Mills and I am certain that will not go well with your superiors?"

The constable lost some of his bravado, his eyes flickering to Alice. "Who is this to you then?"

"She was hired to help me catch those who were stealing from the cargo ships," he stated, his voice hard. It was an easy trick he had learnt from his father.

Since the police hadn't found anything on Alice's person, the constable listened intently to Matthew, the thought of losing his job dawning across his face.

"Then why did ye run?" he asked Alice. "If you were working for him?"

"Because I wanted it to look realistic," she shot back, her eyes flashing. "What else did you expect me to do?"

The constable looked back towards Matthew. He kept his face calm and placid, not allowing his emotions to show through, although inside he was reeling from what he had witnessed tonight. Alice had been stealing. Her wages at the factory hadn't been enough to keep her from stealing the precious cargo. His stomach clenched at the thought of the danger she had subjected herself to and what could have happened if others had learnt that she was a woman and not the young man she had been masquerading as.

"Fine," the constable finally forced out, shoving Alice towards Matthew. She stumbled at the sudden motion and Matthew's hand shot out to catch her, feeling her tremble in his grasp. "But if I find out that something else is amiss here, you can bet you will be seeing me again."

"Then you can find me at the Langford Cotton Mill, on Waldorf Street," Matthew finished, steering Alice away from the constable. It wasn't until he had pushed her inside that he allowed himself to take in a breath. "What were you thinking?" he asked the moment the carriage started moving. "Do not lie to me either, I want the truth."

She couldn't look at him, her eyes transfixed on the drawn curtain over the window. "You weren't supposed to be there tonight."

Matthew let out a harsh laugh. "Are you saying that because I caught you?"

She didn't look in his direction. "The docks are no place for someone like you."

"As they aren't for you, either," he retorted, angry that she would think his life was worth more than hers. "Alice, you put yourself in peril, anything could have happened to you, don't you understand?"

"Why do you care?" she spat out, her eyes now meeting his. He could see the resentment there, but also there was a mixture of wariness, as if she didn't know what he was going to do.

"I'm tired of telling you exactly why I care," he bit out. "That man I saw you with the other day, was he the ringleader?"

Alice looked as if she wasn't going to respond but then she sighed. "Yes, he is. I… I work for him."

A happy relief flitted through Matthew. So, he wasn't her lover but an associate, one of ill repute, too. Despite what he had learnt tonight, nothing had changed about his feelings regarding Alice. "What did he offer you? How much?"

"It doesn't matter," she murmured, breaking her gaze from his. "It was my decision, for the sake of my family, and I'm not sure I would change what I did, even now. You couldn't possibly know what it is like to live in a shanty that threatens to collapse around you on a daily basis. Not everyone is as privileged as you have been, Matthew. We don't just watch the coffers stack up in the bank like you do, never having to worry about a roof over your head or food in your belly."

Her words struck a chord in Matthew, and he heard the desperation in her voice. It wasn't that he had been blind to her living conditions.

"So, if you throw me into prison," she continued bitterly. "The only request I have is that you watch over my father for me."

"Alice I'm not going to hand you over to the police," he murmured, appalled that she would think he could turn her over to the law. "But you will stop this foolishness for the very reason that you gave me just now."

"I was going to end my association with the group tonight anyway. It was going to be my last run. Honest."

Matthew didn't ask her why she had come to that conclusion, but he sincerely hoped that he may be a part of the decision. "I can provide whatever you need," he said quietly as the coach slowed to a stop.

"Alice, please," he started as she reached for the door. He didn't know what to say to her to make her see that he didn't care about where she came from. He only wanted to be part of her future.

She was already opening the door and climbing down the steps, disappearing into the night. Matthew debated going after her, to finish their conversation, but instead he shut the door knocking on the ceiling, sending the coach forward instead.

By the time he reached home, the house was ablaze with light. When he entered, his mother was in the hallway to greet him, still dressed in the gown from earlier. "Where have you been?" she demanded, her mouth twisting as she took in his choice of clothing. "The police have called by."

Of course, they had, probably making sure he was indeed Mr Matthew Langford.

She eyed him. "I am worried about you, Matthew. You haven't been focused lately and there's a nasty rumour that you are paying far too much attention to one of the young ladies at the factory." His mother took a step forward. "Please tell me that it isn't true, Matthew?"

Someone must have seen him with Alice. "Mama, it is true, I have grown attached to someone special."

She reared back as if he had slapped her. She had always been his champion.

"What you say cannot possibly be true," she gasped, her hand at her throat. "Matthew, please, tell me that it isn't so."

"I cannot change how I feel, Mama," he interrupted. "If she will have me, I intend on making her my wife." There. He had said it aloud and it sounded simply perfect to his ears. Alice was all he had ever wanted. None of the fancy women his mother had designs on would ever compare to her inner beauty. She had done what she had to save her family; it didn't diminish the way he felt about her.

His mother huffed but Matthew was already heading up the stairs, he'd had enough this evening, He was exhausted, and he intended to go to bed immediately. Tomorrow, he would meet with Alice and discuss their future together. Matthew shook his head, a smile crossing his face. He had been upset with her about tonight, but he understood why she had taken such measures. She had needed to support her father.

CHAPTER 17

The next few days were agony for Alice. While she didn't want to go to the factory for fear of what might be waiting for her, she knew that she needed the money.

Her father had picked up on her misery and she gave him a halting response, not wanting him to know what she had truly been up to all those nights she had been absent. More importantly, she didn't want him to worry about her.

Being caught by Matthew had made Alice realise that she was truly done with that scurrilous work. They would no longer need the money, now that Matthew had taught her father to read and write.

She was not a bit surprised when Declan found her on her way back from the market, directing her to a side street where they wouldn't be seen. "Bloody hell, Alice," he said, his breath heavy. "I thought I would never see you again. What did that rich feller do to you?"

She gently removed her arm out of his grip. "Nothing. He let me go."

Declan's grin widened. "I can't believe it! How did you manage that?"

She eyed him, looking for any trace of remorse in his gaze and finding none. "Did you not try to seek me out before now?"

"I... I thought that you had been taken to prison already," he protested, his grin fading. "Trust me, Alice. I would have helped if I could."

"No, I'm not sure, you would have," she said softly.

He reached for her, his touch light on her shoulder. "You know, I care for you, lass," he stated. "I didn't want to see you hurt. You must believe me."

Alice was done with Declan and all his empty promises. "I think you do care for me, in your own way," she answered. "But not enough to ensure my safety from the law."

Something akin to hurt flashed across his face before he carefully schooled it behind his jaunty grin. "Well, then," he said finally, shoving his hands in his pockets. "I guess I will have to find myself another partner. Good luck to ye, Alice."

Alice didn't respond, letting him leave instead. Once she'd thought that he might have cared for her, in his own way, but nothing to compare to how Matthew had cared for her since they had played in the garden all those years ago.

Declan had done nothing to stop what could potentially have been disastrous for her, if she hadn't been saved by Matthew.

No there was only one gentleman that she could look to and, surely, he must detest her now. For how could he not?

With a heavy sigh she made her way home. Tomorrow, she would return to the factory and probably she would be required to work out her notice.

Alice entered the factory gates and walked to her loom. Standing there was James Tuckey, the foreman. "Mr Langford would like a word," he stated plainly.

Alice nodded, following James to Matthew's office. Matthew was sitting behind a worn mahogany desk, his dark hair swept back from his forehead, his bright eyes following her every move. There was no trace of emotion on his handsome face. "You may go, James," he informed the foreman. "Please sit, Miss Smythe."

Her knees wobbled as she perched herself on the leather-bound chair in front of the desk, twisting her hands in her lap. What would he say? Was he going to dismiss her now that he knew the worst about her? She had only just informed Declan that she wanted nothing more to do with his outrageous dealings.

What other options would she have if Matthew let her go? She really hadn't given him much of a choice and if others found out about her crimes, then they wouldn't want her in their employ either.

She wouldn't blame him, Alice decided. It wasn't his fault that she had chosen that path.

"I'm sure you are wondering why you are here," he began, resting his elbows on the desk. "I have a great deal I want to understand about your reasoning for stealing from the local businessmen."

"I don't know if I have the answers you are seeking," she admitted. If only she had listened to him all those years ago, how he had tried to tell her that he cared for her. She had been too stubborn to think that he could care enough for someone like her.

Matthew's laugh caught her off guard. "I imagine you don't," he replied, shaking his head. "But I have something to say, regardless."

Alice tried hard to even her breathing. This was it. He was going to dismiss her instantly, then she and her father would be out on the streets in less than a month's time when she had no funds to pay the rent.

Reaching into a drawer, Alice watched as Matthew pulled out a thick stack of what appeared to be letters, tied with a blue satin ribbon. "These are for you," he said softly, pushing them across the desk. "I have written to you over the years, Alice, more than I care to admit. You were the only person that I could cling to during some very dark times in my life, the only one that I knew would listen to me without any judgement."

She didn't know how to respond to that. He had written her, when? She had never received any letters.

"I have a position for you," Matthew continued, his eyes searching hers. "A position that will come with a warm home, and enough food. Your father will have a comfortable room to call his own, with a position in the factory." He cleared his throat. "You will be well cared for."

"What sort of position is that?" she asked breathlessly. This could be all her dreams come true, was he going to offer her the job of maid servant, or even housekeeper, now she could read? Yet she held back from asking.

"You would be my wife," Matthew explained. Alice felt her head become dizzy. His wife? Even after everything she had done, he wished to wed her. How could that be?

"Take the letters," he offered. "You will see that I… well, that my intentions towards you are true."

"Matthew," she inhaled deeply. "I… I…"

"Don't say anything now," he said shaking his head softly. "I don't want you to say yes simply for the treasures I can bring to your life, Alice. I want you to do it because you care for me and me alone. Go home. I will pay your wages for today if you will at least read the letters."

Alice picked up them up. "Yes, I will read them."

Relief flashed across Matthew's face. "Then I will look forward to meeting you afterwards."

Alice walked home in a fog, clutching the letters to her chest. She could scarcely believe that this was what was happening, that Matthew wanted her to be his wife. How could he, she was nowt but a young woman from the East End? Yet when she analysed everything that had happened between them, she could see that over the years they were fated to be together, but she didn't deserve such a good, honest man.

When Alice pushed open the door to the shanty, her father looked up from the book he had been studying. "Alice?" he questioned. "Whatever is wrong? Why are you home at this time of day?" he asked hesitantly.

Tears burned her eyes as she crossed the room and fell to the floor next to his chair, crying softly as he pulled her close. His hand smoothed her hair and he murmured words of comfort until her sobs calmed. "Now," he stated, handing her a kerchief. "Tell me what is amiss, this is not like you."

Alice told him everything, about Matthew, about Declan, and when she quietened, he drew in a breath. "Well, you have yourself in a quandary, my dear gel."

"I don't know what to do, Papa." She sighed, pushing herself off the floor.

He reached for the letters, pushing them gently toward her. "I think you should read these and then decide whether Matthew is your future or not."

Alice drew in a breath as she reached for the pile of letters, giving her father a faint smile before carrying them to her small bed. She still couldn't believe that Matthew had written to her faithfully over the years, even when he had every chance to forget her.

Was that love?

Untying the ribbon, she gingerly lifted the first letter from its envelope, unfolding it. Matthew's scent wafted from the paper and Alice pressed it to her nose, inhaling deeply. She had never truly forgotten about him either, though perhaps her feelings hadn't been as strong as Matthew's.

Now, though, she knew that she could ask for no better person in all of London, to offer her marriage.

Alice unfolded the letter, seeing Matthew's familiar scrawl from their lessons. He had written to her, poured out his feelings on paper for her to read one day.

Today was that day.

She wiped away a tear that trailed down her cheek. It mattered not what these letters said.

Matthew was her future.

Still, Alice settled into reading them, as she had promised Matthew she would before making her decision.

Dearest Alice... she read.

CHAPTER 18

Matthew sat before the fire in his study, a glass of whiskey in his hand left untouched. After his discussion with Alice, he had poured himself into the daily operations of the factory, reviewing ledgers and discussing the changes he wanted to make with his foremen. Then he toured the floors, speaking with the workers and looking for ways to improve their situations both in work and their home environments. They all seemed to appreciate his efforts and for that Matthew felt as if he was making a difference, even slight, to their lives.

Although Alice wasn't far from his mind throughout the day, he wondered what she was thinking regarding his letters—if she was even reading them at all. What if she had thrown them all into the fire, thinking that he was mad for wanting her to read them?

Matthew cringed as he thought of some of the things he had written, clearly a young lad wishing for support from a friend. Would she see him as someone who was looking for a companion or a wife? He knew now without a doubt that he loved Alice. He loved her spirit, the way she had fought for her family and for their survival when it would have been far too easy to just give up.

She had overcome all the demons that had been sent her way and he could think of no one else that he would want by his side, in his future.

To be the mother of his children.

Sighing, he lifted the glass to his lips. His mother was no longer speaking to him, holed up in her own area of the house, which was preferable to him. She would never understand why he could not ever fit in with the life she wanted for him. He had done his duty, and even if Alice was not at his side, he planned to carry on with his work, perhaps even changing the minds of his competitors one day.

That would be his legacy.

The whiskey burned a path to his stomach and Matthew drained the glass before setting it aside. He didn't know how long Alice would wait before giving him an answer, but he hoped it wouldn't be too long. It was taking all his willpower not to make his way over to her shanty, through the dismal rain, to find out what the answer was. He wouldn't go, however. This was her decision, not his. If she did not wish to be his wife, then so be it. He would still give the position to her father and ensure that she was comfortable in his factory for as long as she wished. It did warm his heart that she had no thoughts to go back to her life of crime, and with the additional source of income from her father, she certainly wouldn't have to.

A sudden knock echoed in the hallway, and he listened to the butler open the door before there were rapid steps in his direction. By the time the butler was at the door, Matthew was already out of his chair. "What is it?" he asked hesitantly.

"There's a young woman," the butler announced and sniffed haughtily. "At the door, requesting to speak to you."

"Then show her in!" Matthew shot back; his voice harsher than he intended it to be. The butler turned to do his bidding and Matthew strode to the sitting room door, pulling it wide open to catch a glimpse of a rain-soaked Alice making her way to him. "Get some towels, quickly," he called out, pulling her gently into the warm study. "You are freezing."

"It is a long walk," she stammered, her teeth chattering together.

With a curse, Matthew moved her to the fireplace, stripping off her sodden gloves so that he could massage some feeling back into her hands. "You are so stubborn," he bit out as his fingers worked over her rough ones. If she caught the ague for this, he would never forgive himself. "Walking out in the rain like that!"

"Matthew," she protested but he ignored her, stopping long enough to accept the towels from the butler before wrapping one around her quaking shoulders. He had to get her warm before she fell ill.

Rubbing her with the towel briskly, he tried to soak the water out of her coat before cursing and stripping the coat off itself, finding her dress plastered to her skin.

Her hands found his and she forced him to look at her. "Stop."

Matthew paused. "At least let me get you a whiskey."

"Please," Alice replied. "I will be fine for a few moments. I… I need to speak with you."

Matthew draped the towel over her shoulders. "All right."

She clenched the towel, drawing in a breath. "I read your letters."

Matthew started. "And what did you think?" he asked thickly, steeling himself for whatever came next. If she didn't see how much he cared, then he would have to accept it.

A smile flitted across her expression. "I confess, I couldn't read some of the words, but it didn't take me long to see what I needed to. They were… they were lovely, Matthew."

"That is because you are lovely," he murmured, reaching up to cup her cheek with his hand. "Alice, I don't know what to say. I don't know how to express myself in words, but as you can tell, I am able to write my feelings for you on paper." It was true, what he felt for her, he couldn't put into words.

She stepped closer, her own hands framing his face. "I don't deserve you," she started. "You deserve a well-bred, fine lady, one that you can have on your arm and proudly acknowledge that she is your wife."

"But she won't be you," he forced out. "I don't want that kind of woman on my arm, Alice. I want one that will challenge me, one that will laugh with me." His hands slid to her waist, and he boldly pulled her closer, until there were mere inches between them. "I want a wife who cares for me and not my status or my money. I want one who will help me improve our factory and raise our children the right, empathetic way, to not see social statuses but real people."

A tear slipped down her cheek, and he gave her a tender smile. "And I believe that woman is you, Alice."

"Matthew," she breathed. "This cannot be real."

He leant down, brushing his lips over hers. How many times had he imagined himself doing just that? "It is," he whispered, pressing his forehead against hers.

They stood there before the fire, drinking in the closeness of each other until Alice finally spoke. "I will marry you, Matthew. I… I love you."

Matthew pulled her close, burying his face in her wet hair. She had said yes. She wanted to be his wife.

His future, his hopes, would be secure with her by his side.

After a few moments, Alice pulled away, her cheeks flushed from either the heat or their closeness, he wasn't certain which. "Well, what now?" she asked.

"First, I need to purchase an engagement ring," he replied with a smile. "Then you will need to pick a date for us to wed, and I do hope it will be soon."

"And my father?" Alice asked, her eyes on his.

"Nothing has changed, Alice," he murmured. "Your father will have a position in the factory, and I will continue with his lessons and yours."

His home would be filled with love and laughter once more and though he knew it would come as a shock to his mother, she would eventually come to accept it or leave. It mattered not to him, only that he would be happy, and that Alice would be happy.

"Whatever did I do to deserve you?" she whispered softly, tears filling her eyes.

He tipped her chin upward, leaning down to kiss her again…

CHAPTER 19

TWO YEARS LATER...

lice reached into the barrow and pulled out the milk and bread, handing it to the young girl. "Make certain you finish it all," she replied as the girl clutched the precious supplies to her thin chest. "This will help you feel stronger throughout the day."

"Yes, miss," the girl replied before moving through the factory entrance. Alice watched her go before pulling some more goods out of the barrow, handing it the next person in line. Both were precious commodities to their workers, but they provided it daily, even sending some home at the end of the week so that they may share it with their loved ones. The idea had come from Matthew, finding out that if the workers were well fed, then they tended to be less sick, and therefore able to be better able to work with less accidents.

Alice couldn't remember the last time they'd had an accident in the factory, a veritable feat indeed.

"What are you doing, my love?"

Alice turned at the sound of her husband's voice, giving him a small smile. "Matilda was feeling under the weather today so I told her I would take her position."

Matthew joined her, gently pulling out the next portion himself. "You shouldn't be doing such a chore. I fully expected you to still be in bed at this hour."

"Then I'm not sure you have learnt anything about me these past two years," she teased as he handed the supplies to the next in line. "You know I am not one to laze around in bed."

Her husband leant in close to her ear. "Unless I am keeping you there, my love," he answered cheekily.

Despite being wed for two years, Alice still flushed at his strongly suggestive words. "Go on with you! We have work to complete."

He chuckled but didn't leave and together they were able to move the line along quickly. Once the barrow was empty, her father joined them, a clipboard in his hand. "That's all of them," he announced, signing his name with flourish.

"Excellent," Matthew replied, sliding his hand around Alice's waist. "Another successful day of everyone coming to work."

Alice gave him a smile. Matthew had been experimenting with different ways to reduce the sickness amongst his factory workers lately, providing a series of food baskets to see if he could improve their health and that of their loved ones. So far, it had worked, and he was due to present his findings to the businessman's forum at the end of the month. She was so proud of him and how he genuinely cared about those that kept them in a comfortable home, but more importantly, she loved him for his heart. Matthew was the kindest, gentlest person she knew, and her life would not be complete without him.

"Well, now," Matthew said, guiding Alice towards the house. "I think it's time for you to prop your feet up in front of the fire and do nothing but rest for the remainder of the day."

Alice laughed, tucking her hand around his waist. Ever since he had found out that she was carrying his heir, he had been impossible, and she almost dreaded the months ahead from his nagging. "Come now, Mr Langford, your wife is far from fragile."

He winked at her. "That I know but you are still my wife and I want you to do as I say."

She arched a brow as they walked through the front door, the smells of delicious cooking heavy in the air. "When have I ever done what you have asked of me?"

"Never," he teased, placing a kiss on her forehead. "Which is why I love you."

Her resolve melted and she leant against him, stifling a yawn. "Perhaps you are right," she admitted as he steered her toward the dining room where she knew a small feast would be laid out. "I have been growing tired much quicker these days."

Matthew smiled and her heart clenched at the sight. Even his mother had come around to the fact that he had wed someone from the East End, though it had been a trial to begin with. Once Alice had shown her that she loved Matthew fiercely, it hadn't been hard to have her accept their marriage.

What a wedding it had been! Instead of a room full of people they didn't know, Matthew had invited the factory workers to join them in the factory, plying them with more than enough food for them and their families. Then, after a honeymoon in Scotland, interrupted by a visit to Uncle Winston and Aunt Lucinda, they had both returned, refreshed and ready to make their factory the most productive one in the whole of London.

Now, Alice felt as if they were truly on their way.

Matthew pulled out a chair and Alice seated herself on it, smiling when she felt his lips brush over her temple. "Do you know what day it is, my love?" he asked lightly as he joined her at the table.

She arched a brow. "Why, it is Thursday."

"That it is," he replied, pulling his napkin over his lap. "It was a Thursday the day that I first fell in love with you."

Alice let out a laugh, remembering his stories well. "That little scruffy urchin, you mean. What a sight I must have been."

"You were more than that," he said with a wink. "You gave a lonely little boy attention and that was all it took for me to fall for you that day."

Alice flushed as she reached over, clenching his hand in hers. No matter how many times he had told her about his great love for her, it was hard to believe that this was her life now. It had nothing to do with the amount of funds they had, or the fact that she never had to worry about the roof over her head or enough food to eat.

No, it had to do with the quiet nights before the fire, where she pored over books, with stories she never imagined she would be able to read. Sometimes, Matthew read to her, with Alice nestled in his lap listening to the steady beat of his heart. It was also the mornings where she opened her eyes to find him watching her as she slept, love reflecting in his expression.

She didn't know what the future was going to bring, but this child, and the others that would surely follow, would forever be surrounded by love.

"I confess I didn't love you then," she teased. "But now I love you even more than I could possibly imagine."

~*~*~

Thank you so much for reading my story.

If you enjoyed reading this book may I suggest that you might also like to read my recent release 'Emma's Forlorn Hope' next which is available on Amazon for just £0.99 or free with Kindle Unlimited.

Click Here to Get Your Copy Today!

Sample of First Chapter

Rain fell hard against the windowpanes, the thick splatters sounding like gunshots in the quiet and dark of the house. Though it was day, the ashen grey clouds blanketed the world like a death shroud. There was a chill in the air, a driving wind clawing its way through the cracks in the stonework and whistling like angered banshees through the house. The raging elements made it hard to think and Emma Moss could not have been more thankful for it. Thinking was the last thing she wanted, as was silence. For the last two days, the house had been quiet as the grave and she could hardly stand it. Angry though the elements were, their raging cacophony was welcome to the nothingness that had taken over her home.

Sat in the rocking chair at her mother's bedside, Emma stared blankly at the windows, watching them rattle whilst trying to count each raindrop. Dark rings circled her eyes and her cheeks were stained with the dried-up channels of tears that no longer flowed. Wrapped in an old, frayed shawl, Emma barely noticed the cold. She was far too numb.

By her side, Emma's mother lay silent and quiet in the bed, covered in as many layers of blankets as Emma could find about the house. She would have had a fire going, except water had gotten to the logs. She hadn't bothered to complain to Father. Since Mother had fallen ill, the man had come undone. Though never very reliable to begin with, Thomas Moss was nothing without his wife. He was a boat and she the rudder. Emma was told it had always been so, and that her father would never have amounted to anything in life without her mother's influence. Now, as the woman they both loved lay silent and dying in her bed, Emma felt she truly understood the kind of man her father was. Content to wallow in ennui and self-pity, he had holed himself away in the quiet corners of the house for the past days, never once looking to cook for or check after his children. Emma had to ride out to the wet nurse in the nearby village to beg her care for her young sister for a few days, and she was glad she had done so. If left under her father's watch, Emma was certain baby Mary would have been left to starve.

As dissatisfied thoughts of her father swirled through her head, Emma let out a sigh. She tried to ignore the dark and empty fireplace and instead thought about slipping beneath the covers of her mother's bed. Their combined warmth would do them both good, she thought.

With nothing to be done until dinner and the doctor's next visit, Emma made up her mind. Rising up from the chair, the floor creaked loudly underfoot as she moved around the bed and slipped beneath the patchwork covers. She had hoped she was quiet enough not to disturb her mother's rest, but she felt a stirring beneath the sheets as she lay down next to the woman who had raised and nurtured her.

"Thomas… Is that you? Finally risked coming back to your own bed?"

"No, Mama, it's me," Emma spoke softly. She heaved a sigh as she turned her head into the pillows. She wanted to apologise for her father never being there, but it was not her crime to apologise for.

"Your father still sitting in the living room? If he's not careful he'll run out of chances to see me," Mrs Moss said, her voice a pitiful whisper.

"Don't speak like that Mother," Emma said, pushing in a little closer and wrapping her arms around the woman who had raised her.

"Where's Mary?" Mrs Moss asked, before descending into a fit of coughing. Emma sat up and passed over a pewter cup of water. Her mother swallowed a few grateful sips then coughed again.

As Emma took back the glass, she could not help but notice the flecks of blood on the rim of the cup. "Where's Mary?" the woman asked again.

"I told you last time you woke, I sent her to Elsie Brown, the wet nurse. She's promised to look after Mary at no charge until you get better."

"Does she know that'll mean adopting her?" Mrs Moss asked, her gallows humour earning no laugh from her daughter.

The room fell to silence once more, mother and daughter both lying wrapped up together and listening to the sound of the driving rain. Emma held her mother tight in her arms, possessively.

"You know you can't afford to be like your father," Emma heard her mother say, her voice softer.

"Mother?"

"You can't keep going through life finding ways to pretend everything is fine when the house is burning down around you."

"I don't think there is any chance of that with all this rain," Emma joked, trying desperately to deflect her mother's message.

"You know what I mean, Emma," her mother said. She turned now, staring into her eldest daughter's eyes. It was the most alert and together she had seemed in days and yet Emma felt a shudder pass through her as she studied her mother's face. It was so sallow, her skin like paper hanging off her bones. Her hair was limp and lifeless, and she just seemed exhausted—thoroughly and completely. "I want to know that you will look after Mary," the woman continued. There was an edge to her voice, her request one that Emma could not dismiss or bat aside with empty assurances.

"Will you look after Mary when I am gone, Emma?" her mother asked again. Beneath the sheets, her hands moved to find her daughter's, winding their fingers together and grasping tight. "I need to know that you won't abandon her or let anything bad happen to her. I… I love your father, but I know what he is like, too. He won't be any good at all when I'm gone. I need to know I can rely on you to look after yourself and your sister."

Emma bit her bottom lip. She thought she was done with crying. In the last days she had shed so many tears she felt certain she had nothing left to give. Still, as she tried to summon up the words to answer her mother, she felt the familiar dampness on her cheeks, the hateful blurring at the edges of her vision. She couldn't refuse to answer her mother, at the same time she wanted so desperately to ignore the question. Emma couldn't explain it, but she felt at that moment as if she had the power over life and death with her answer. It felt like her mother was asking for her permission to die, ready to slip away once Emma gave her the assurance that she needed to enter that last and deepest of rests.

"Mother, I…"

"Please, Emma," the woman begged again, her dull eyes staring intently at her.

"You know I won't let anything happen to Mary," Emma said at last. The words were halting, broken between half sobs as she nestled into her mother and rested her head in the crook of her neck.

"That's my good girl," came a voice that seemed eerily peaceful and distant. Emma took deep lungfuls of air as she tried to calm herself. No further words passed between them. Emma did not know what else to say, only able to communicate her feelings by the way she held fast to her mother in the dark.

∾

HER EYES FLICKERED OPEN. Outside, the rain had eased to a dull drizzle and the wind calmed to a respectful whisper. It was later than Emma had expected it to be. The bedroom was swathed in darkness and there was no light from under the door frame. The dark clouds of day had drawn into a night, black as pitch, and Emma could hardly even make out her mother's form in the bed. Even without sight, Emma felt something was wrong.

Her mother was still, her body limp in a way that didn't feel like sleep. Emma's hand ran down her mother's arm, moving to her wrist to check for a pulse. For a moment, Emma's whole body tensed, and her lips pursed with worry. Her eyes stared into the dark ahead of her, unfocused and empty as she confirmed her suspicions.

Although there had been weeks to prepare and days to contemplate the possibility of her mother's death, Emma had put it off. Lying next to the unmoving and silent body, she felt as if she should feel something. She should start to cry again, wrap her arms about her mother and hold her as grief took over. Those felt like the right and natural things to do, but Emma found no compulsion or desire to do either.

Instead, she sat up. Sat up and pulled herself out of bed, taking a moment to light the nearby candle on the bedside table. In the faint illumination, she busied herself. She straightened the bed sheets and turned her mother so that she lay flat on her back with hands clasped together over her chest. This done, Emma found her shoes and slipped them on.

Stepping out into the hall, the girl found no light shining anywhere in the house. She held the candle in her hand firmly as she walked through to the living area and kitchen. There was a weak two-day-old broth in one of the pans left for them to eat. It was not much, but it would do until she could go out to the town in the morning. Finding the last of the coal in the kitchen, Emma set about lighting the stove, making a mental note of all that would need doing the next day.

There was the undertaker to inform and the parish priest. Doctor Philips would also need to know, and as Emma thought of the man, she wondered why he had not called as agreed. It did not matter much she told herself, focussing on what food she would need to purchase. How long could she leave Mary in the care of Mrs Brown? She had no doubt the kindly wet nurse would agree to look after her baby sister as long as was needed, but Emma couldn't take advantage of that generosity. Besides, she had promised mother that she would see to Mary.

The ongoing list of duties, responsibilities and plans marched on through Emma's mind as she stirred up the old broth in the pan. She stared into the liquid, hardly noticing as a shadow moved behind her. Only when the corner chair creaked did she realise her father had walked in. No doubt he could smell the food.

"How is she?" came the tentative question.

Emma almost didn't want to answer. She wasn't looking to spare her father's feelings or avoid the topic. Instead, she felt as though he had no right to know what had happened. He had chosen to lock himself away the last days and nights, resolutely shuttering the world out to wallow in self-pity. He didn't deserve to know anything. If he wanted to know he should march into his bedroom and see for himself.

"She's dead," Emma answered simply, knowing it would do no good to indulge in petty revenge. She stopped stirring the broth in the pan for a moment, listening for any sign of life or emotion behind her.

She did not turn around though, not wishing to look her father in the eyes.

"Was it quick?" The man's voice was weak when he spoke, but Emma heard it.

"I don't know. I know she had fallen asleep. I closed my eyes to rest and when I woke again, she was gone." There was no emotion in her voice, just facts; as if she was telling the news of someone wholly unrelated to her.

For a few minutes, all was silent. Father said nothing, and Emma could not hear him stirring from his chair behind her. She continued with the cooking, stirring the remaining soup until it was bubbling hot. She then dished the meagre meal into two bowls and carried them over to the table. One she lay down before her father, not even looking him in the eyes as she did so. The other, she took to her own place.

"I'll need to see several people in town tomorrow," Emma said, her voice wooden and mechanical. "You'll need to see about going back to work soon. I can't look after Mary and go out to wash and clean for the Parr family."

"We'll move to the city," Thomas said, his voice matter of fact and strangely resolute. He too seemed numbed by everything, left empty and emotionless.

"The city?" Emma sucked in a breath, feeling a twinge of uncertainty. "Why would you say that?"

"It's where the work is," Thomas replied. "I can't expect to get anything here, not after what happened around the time your mother fell ill. Besides, I don't much feel like staying on in this place."

Emma took a sip of soup between pursed lips. "Do you know what you'd do in London?" she asked, trying to put on that voice her mother used to keep a check on him.

"I'll find something," he said, following the words up with a too-casual shrug.

And that was the end of it. Both numb, both unwilling or unable to grieve as they should, father and daughter ate their meal in silence, with the prospect of a new start in the city added to Emma's fears and uncertainties for the future…

~*~*~

This wonderful Victorian Romance story —
'Emma's Forlorn Hope' — is available on Amazon
for just £0.99 or *FREE* with Kindle Unlimited
simply by clicking on the link below.

**Click Here to Get Your Copy of 'Emma's Forlorn
Hope' - Today!**

A NOTE FROM THE AUTHOR

Dear Reader,

Thank you so much for choosing and reading my story — I sincerely hope it lived up to your expectations and that you enjoyed it as much as I loved writing about the Victorian era.

This age was a time of great industrial expansion with new inventions and advancements.

However, it is true to say that there was a distinct disparity amongst the population at that time — one that I like to emphasise, allowing the characters in my stories to have the chance to grow and change their lives for the better.

Best Wishes
Ella Cornish

Newsletter

If you love reading Victorian Romance stories…

**Simply sign up here and get your FREE copy of
The Orphan's Despair**

Click Here to Download Your Copy - Today!

More Stories from Ella!

If you enjoyed reading this story you can find more great reads from Ella on Amazon…

Click Here for More Stories from Ella Cornish

Contact Me

If you'd simply like to drop us a line you can contact us at **ellacornishauthor@gmail.com**

You can also connect with me on my Facebook Page **https://www.facebook.com/ellacornishauthor/**

I will always let you know about new releases on my Facebook page, so it is worth liking that if you get the chance.

LIKE Ella's Facebook Page **_HERE_**

I welcome your thoughts and would love to hear from you!

Printed in Great Britain
by Amazon

78450335R00111